ISBN-13: 9781969239007
ISBN-10: 196923900X

Cover image by: A L Watson
with additional design work by: A S H
Printed in the United States of America

I0662512

TWISTING THE TURALL

Book 4 Empathy

A S H

OTHER BOOKS BY THE AUTHOR

A White Rabbit in Summer

Lovelife of a Deathdealer

Twisting The Turall

Ether

Voyage

Gold

Empathy

CONTENTS

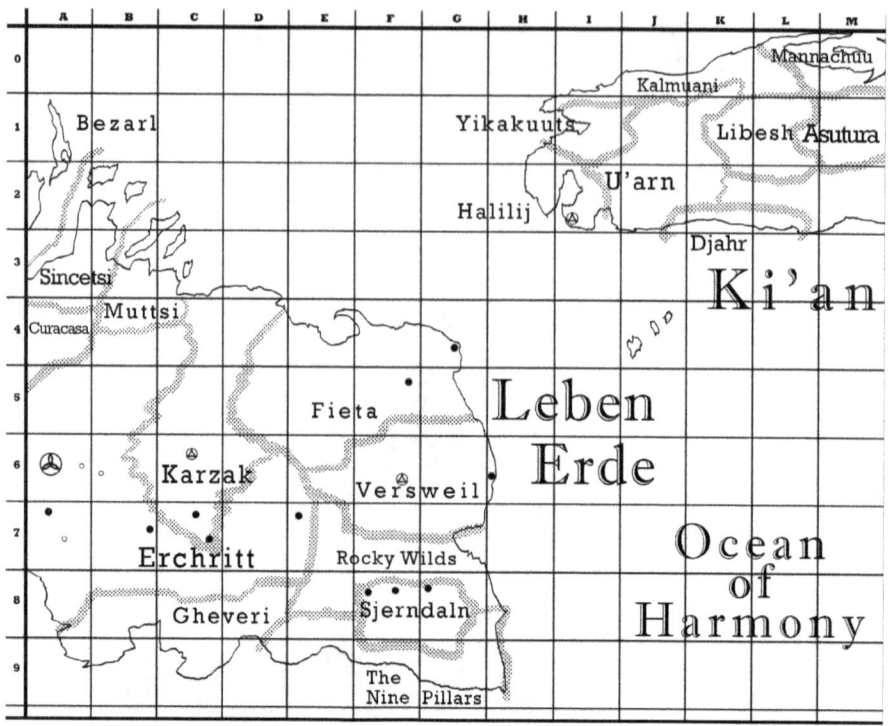

Cities and Notable Locations

==

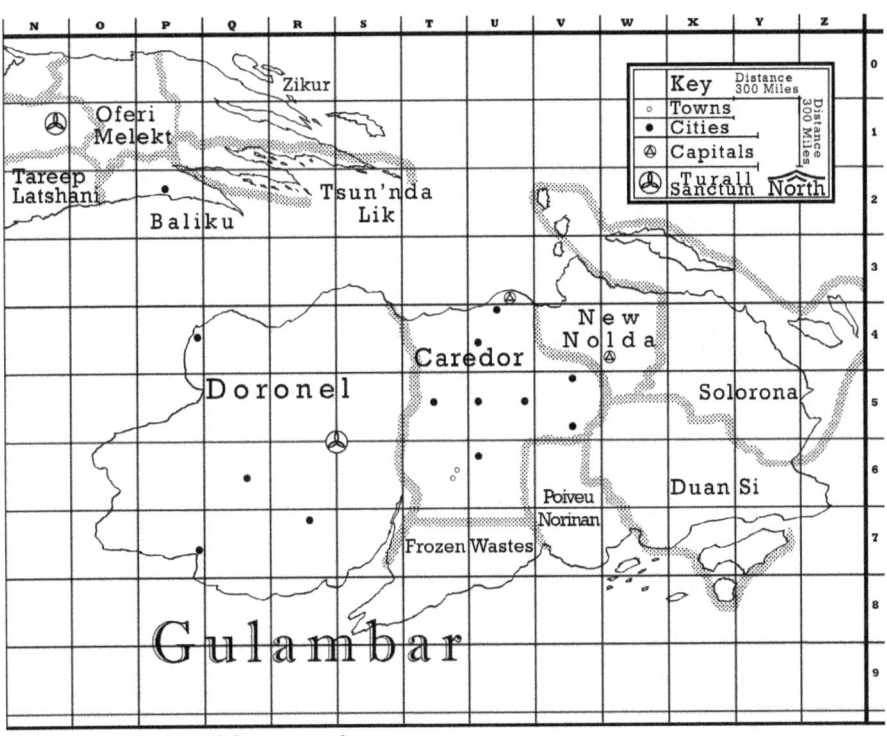

Cities and Notable Locations

==

THE STORY THUS FAR

Every few generations the Turall are reborn to bring about the Grand Dream, a world changing war where the transman warrior, Hultur, conquers Gulambar, imprisons the albino queen, Ngoltur, and is defeated by the hero, Muttur.

The Gods chose Ngoltur to be **Ena** an antisocial girl dispised by her parents, the exiled King and Queen of Doronel. Hiding her natural power, she grew up as an outcast among the ambitious ladder climbers of Caredor.

Upon graduation Ena became a Broker, a kind of rural problem solver. She worked under the guidance of Captain **Torno**, an infamous scoundrel of the Great Generation. Ena had known his love from a Romantic Escape where the user could live as his girlfriend **Kalta**.

Knowing Torno couldn't be trusted, Ena kept to herself, but slowly came to be friends with her coworkers:

Narla, a grenadier haunted by the revolution.

Visk, a giant Ki'an warrior who lost the love of her life.

Sal, a rock-human Boulba construction worker.

Myrrel, a noble-born healer with vitiligo.

On Ena's birthday, she meets **Hultur** Reborn. Though taking the name of the ancient conqueror, Hultur insists that he's on a mission of peace. Ena and her friends all agree to accompany him to Leben Erde, where they hope to find Muttur, and end the Grand Dream peacefully.

Ena says goodbye to a kind man, Haenir, giving him a night of love to make up for the life they were denied. In the sleep of love, she received a vision of his death, being killed by two Ki'an warriors and Leben boy with red eyes.

Reaching Sothlen in the middle of an attack by a mega monster, Ena unleashes her full power to destroy the mega in a single attack. A formal inquiry is done by **Cerrano** and **Iodize**, two incompetent Junior Mages who vow to keep their eye on him.

Promoted for his act of heroism, Torno uses the ceremony to kill Magus Yersen and start a revolution. The Brokers have to flee as fugitives. The Junior Mages track Torno all the way to the capital and Torno is injured in an escape from his ex, the Archmage Kalta.

Aboard the Endless Grace, Torno's condition is critical. Narla takes command and assigns each of the Brokers with a task to prepare Ena for the fighting to come. Ena makes herself battle ready, studies Ki'an magic, identifies emotional nodes, learns healing magic, and advanced techniques.

Endless Grace is captained by **Fascinosa**, a fish-man and exiled prince of an underwater kingdom. The ship is full of fish-human Marinelds, including the young exiled Princess Titiarna. **Teetee** and Ena become quick friends, sharing secrets in her cabin.

Seeing this bond wish his surrogate daughter, Fascinosa tries to woo Ena with secret letters.

Hultur creaties a magical rug of haste, where she can study sixty times faster. Ena tries to master ether control in one year, but her sanity wavers after three months. Shaken but stronger she tries finding solace in Fascinoa's arms only to learn he is looking for love not sex.

Accepting her destiny as Ngoltur Reborn, she takes command of the crew from Narla and disembarks for Endless Grace with Fascinosa's blessing. He wishes them luck and asks that they care for **Zukoch**.

A Leben deckhand native to Fieta, Zukoch had a series of encounters with the crew that no one remembers. But he knows the city of Vergebaum Heffe well enough to find them room and board.

Hoping to work out some of her frustration, Ena hooks up with a Ki'an mercenary and divorcee, **Obi**. The next day she runs into Obi who takes her to Kalta. He and his mercanry company, the Twin Eagles, have signed on to work with the Archmage. Kalta offers Torno amnesty overseas and pardons for Ena and everyone else, all she has to do is capitulate to her will. Ena sees through her false offer and flees the city.

A threat unique to the continent of Leben Erde are the Reptear, lizard-people made by Doronel casters. Designed to destroy monsters they instead figured out a way to tame monsters and live alongside them.

A threat too large to eradicate, Fieta leaves many uncivilized lands to rashes of Reptear. The Black Tooth Woods are one such source of the lizard-people. Pursued by Kalta and the Junior Mages, Ena risks entering the Reptear lands. It is in the Black Tooth Woods they encounter a human child working with the Reptear, a Cannegurin. In a fit of rage, Ena handles the problem.

Talking to the Dreamers of Fieta, they learn that most Dreamers are nothing more than figureheads, that only the Grand Dreamer might know what the Gods have planned for Ena and Hultur.

Kalta and Obi have anticipated Ena's path and an army of hundreds of Fieta mercenaries and Caredor casters ride to kill Ena. She lures Kalta's army towards a lake. Calling upon her deep well of power, Ena swirls the lake and uses it as a weapon. Though successful, the attack sends her into an ether coma where she sees a vision of an ice wall collapsing.

Recovered and safe in the Boulba nation of Karzak, Torno shares the truth of his past with Kalta to the group. It is a story Ena didn't know in full. Kalta and Torno were once in love, but her cruel nature drove him away and when he finally left her for good she used her parents access as the propoganda arm of the Supreme Magus to turn the nation of Caredor against Torno. Though wronged by Kalta, Torno admits that he did a lot of terrible things as her lover and he asks for no forgiveness.

Traveling south down Karzak's great Boulba highway, word of Ena's destiny has spread. All in Karzak know she is Ngoltur Reborn and she is welcome at the capital of Ozalto as a hero. Presented gifts by the nations many Senators, she receives a magical necklace by her Grand Uncle, the exiled Prince **Yeldo** Noiru Vamqinsys.

Rumors were that Yeldo was exiled for his love of a man, but he bore children and was actually banished for wanting to grant powers to the lower class. He has connections in Doronel set to establish Ena as the rightful Queen, demolishing the democracy that has existed her entire life. Leaning on her love for her friends, he talks her into being a figurehead to unite Gulambar.

Pitched this idea of making Ena Queen, her friends balk. Sal suspects the magical necklace and Hultur, Zukoch, and Torno are able to identify the empathy spells woven to influence Ena's mind. Confronting Yeldo, he admits to using magic to control her, but begs her to go through with the plan to make her Queen. The stress of his failure kills his aged heart.

Rejecting her crown, the Gods take notice.

Shown a secret exit by the elected ruler of Karzak, Ena and her Aides travel through the lava tunnels of a volcano. On the other side of Karzak, they have a straight shot towards a Treasury of the Grand Dream, and on the flat top mountain entrance they see a young Leben boy running up to the top: Muttur.

Ena feels time alter without any apparent cause. On their way to meet Muttur, that sensation gets stronger and stronger, until at last they talk to him. Only Muttur doesn't speak back, he walks along their ranks, looking at each of them until a monster attacks and in that moment of distraction he guts Narla, flips out of the reach of Visk's attack, and shoots Myrrel in the neck.

Doing everything Ena can to save Myrrel, it isn't enough, and Myrrel has to abandon saving Narla to save her own life. Muttur escapes and everyone grieves the death of Narla.

Hoping to send the Gods a message, they cremate Narla with an explosion that destroys a Treasury of the Grand Dream. Knowing that Muttur is their true enemy, they head to Erchritt to meet the Grander Dreamer.

THE FORTY-FIFTH CHAPTER

When Silence Reigns

Raindrops pattered onto the roof of the stable. It had been a long day of hard riding for Ngoltur and her Aides. Only Gale was unphased by the day's march. He was looking to Ena with anticipation and hope, but the rain prohibited her from taking him out for one of her contemplative jaunts. Nothing was going how Ena wanted, this talk with her Aides would be as pointless as the others. She longed to get back to Myrrel's book on healing and the tomb of time full of secrets.

"I want a wagon," Hultur said for the tenth time since they watched Rookt Monte's end.

"It's slower," Ena said with a shake of her head. "Besides, I don't even know if we can afford one."

Narla used to handle finances. Since that time the job had fallen to Torno, who felt it necessary to allocate a certain amount of funds to always having a barrel of wine or gin, which only Torno seemed to like. Since the purchase of that barrel of gin, Ena had taken over finances. Besides which, Torno was drinking too much. A few of them were. They didn't know how to balance their drinking like Ena did. Two drinks at the end of the day just to settle down and sleep. And another two if they happened to be at a proper bar, but only so she could relax and dance with the locals.

"I want to try being a counselor again," Sal told the group. "I know that things didn't work well with Ena the first time, but I did take time to make a plan on how to improve my methods and

I have some ideas."

His speech was slurring. He'd been drinking that refined oil while they rode. Patches, the hated horse that survived Muttur's attack, the useless beast that couldn't even be bothered to mourn his rider, had been weighed down carrying oil and wine for too long. He and his misshapen ankle were slowing the group down. Ena had wanted to trade him for a new horse, but much of Erchritt didn't have horses. Instead, they filled up their stables with the ostrich-like Schistrau.

Feathered beasts unnerved Ena. Every small change in their environment was an excuse for the floofy Schistrau to pop up their mane of feathers or squawk. They were loud, ornery things that smelled of flower and flour. They all came in fancy colors and their riders charged far too much to exchange them besides. The people of Erchritt were obsessed with schistrau. Every bar, tavern, inn, city hall, and marketplace they'd been to always had someone playing the lively Schistrau's Song. It was an obnoxious earworm with a melody so lively it outright denied conversation, not that Ena found many that knew any Dorospek.

"Ena?" Sal asked.

It was so hard for Ena to concentrate in this boring country of Erchritt.

"I don't see why not," she said. "I'm having trouble grabbing onto my nodes anyway."

"You weren't listening." Torno took a drag. He was better that way, with his cigarette silencing all of his dumb comments.

"I'm listening now and I said he could counsel me again."

"Ena, he wants to try counseling everyone," Myrrel pointed out.

"Yeah, why not. Zukoch having some nodes couldn't hurt," she said, quickly. She was itching to get to her nightly drinks and book reading.

Zukoch had been trying to learn offense magic and after a paragraph long incantation coupled with an energetic flailing of his wand, he was capable of creating a spark about the size of a cup. The boy had no head for magic and even less ether. He could output maybe three gulda in a day. If he wasn't such a good cook, Ena would've told him to fuck off. She wanted all of them to fuck off. They'd be better off settling down in a little town like this.

"Ena?" Myrrel asked like she'd just said something.

Ena stood up. "Listen, I'm just tired. What's the problem with Sal counseling people?"

"There's no one to counsel me," he said again.

They were losing their patience with her and the feeling was mutual.

"I'll do it. Anything else?" She scanned the group. Torno had something he wanted to say, but he took a drag instead. "Good. I'll see you all tomorrow morning."

Ena walked into the light drizzle to go around the inn and find where people drank. Oraus Groon was a town as forgettable as it was hard to navigate. People lived where they worked and the many businesses were connected by a baffling sprawl of dirt paths. The inn was an abomination, separated from a tavern or even a dining hall. The building was more or less in total isolation at the edge of town. This seemed to be the Erchritt way. Nothing was convenient, everything required a long conversation that Ena couldn't follow, so she inevitably had to stand there and smile while these locals gabbed at her for minutes on end. It was an inconvenience that baffled the mind, but most of Erchritt baffled the mind.

Erchritt, as a people, seemed to hate drinking and their templeless religion was confusing and prohibitive. Something like a pantheon existed on a hierarchy and individual towns had patron gods that watched over them. A small village like Oraus Groon might have four or five individual patrons, some were people that had once lived. She'd picked up enough Faulchet to talk about simple things, but so many of their idioms were connected with their confounding religion.

Torno ran to catch up with her. Apparently, the town's layout wasn't confusing enough.

"Oh, good. Torno is here, the counselor I never asked for. All of my problems will be righted because Torno has something so important he can't even bring it up during the nightly meetings." Ena laid on the sarcasm thick as the mud in this tree covered blight.

"Can you shut those cheeks long enough to listen to me or are you determined to treat every problem with the seriousness of a fart?" he grumbled.

Ena made a fart noise.

"There's talk of changing leaders."

Ena took refuge from the light rain under a tree. "That's important enough. Who's floating the idea?"

Torno shook his head. "Not the point. A lot of us are worried about you and your nightly habits."

"Drinking," she laughed. "You have the audacity to talk to me about how much I'm drinking? How much gin did you drink on the road today? Or did you really think that I didn't notice you taking sips every time you had to go off to relieve yourself? Alcohol makes you pee more. It would be slowing us down if Myrrel and Visk weren't right there with you. At least I have the decency to wait until we're done traveling. We done now?"

"Not really, no. Because it isn't just the drinking. I know about the rug."

"And you've come to congratulate me for overcoming my fears, that's very big of you, Torno." She could see the lights of a hunter's lodge. String instruments sang inside. Meat lured her senses to the distant orange glow behind the trees.

Torno stepped in front of her, his eyes doing that annoying *you can trust me* curl. "What fears?"

"I was afraid of the rug of haste but now I'm not. Now I can squeeze in a day or two to learn more healing magic every night. Or did you want another person to die because I can't heal as well as Myrrel?"

Torno looked away.

"No? Good. Kindly fuck off and let me relax."

"It's making you erratic, Ena. You're different. You can barely follow a conversation," he said like he had to walk on eggshells around her.

"Oh, I can't?" She made a fake pout. "Maybe you're not that interesting, Torno. Did you ever consider that?"

"Of course," he scowled.

"It's been a long day. I just want to have a few drinks with these locals before I go back to my time rug and get some real work done. If you fuckers want to stage a coup, fine, but know that while all of you are having secret meetings, I'm learning two high magicks and a new language. I'm the one doing real good and actually trying to find a way to kill Muttur. But, yeah, go ahead and stage a coup. I'm sure it'll help the group."

He ran off to drink his gin and stroke his tiny little dick.

Ena gave a sigh to steady herself. It was getting harder and harder to deal with them; him in particular. She walked up and knocked on the door to the hunter's lodge.

A gruff Leben man with a full beard asked in Faulchet, "Can I help you?"

"Here to drink," she said in his airy language.

He said something Ena didn't understand and shut the door. Locals only? Fuck this village. Whatever. She had enough whiskey in her flask to get her to sleep inside the circle. With all of their talk about coups maybe Ena should be spending more time in the circle. If they saw her getting bigger results they wouldn't care so much about her spending all this time alone.

The key to Ena's new system was accepting that she lost time to go to the privy and relieve herself and to be okay walking around with no clothes at all. Washing slowed her down. These rooms never had showers or baths anyway. They didn't even have proper plumbing most of the time. She always had to go out to some pond or water spigot to wash herself. It was a waste of time and washing raised far too much suspicion from these superstitious Erchritt.

About four days into her night's studies, she was walking naked to the privy and spotted flames outside. The rain had stopped, but it should still be too wet for fires to spread. Still, she had gone out to take a shit and couldn't exactly put that off. Haste solved everything. She had spent too long being afraid of her power. Now that she wasn't a scared little girl, she could move around in a haste bubble without blubbering like an animal.

Ena walked out of her private room and saw the dorsal crests of Reptear illuminated by flames consuming the hunter's lodge. Darkness kept Ena from pinpointing the lizard men, but that was nothing a little magic couldn't fix. Three gestures ended with her making a three fingered figure slithering in the air. A snake of pure light manifested between the trees. Even after the attack on the lodge, these crafty Reptear had infested the woods. They were crawling around to get in close and devour Ena, but they looked pretty silly now.

A change of state shifted the ether from harmless light to crackling lightning. One by one the electric snake flew through the lizard-people. One single arrow traveled through the distance. Stopped in mid air, Ena took the time to lung back in mock pain, holding at her heart and sticking out her tongue. Twisting her hand around, the arrow tuned back to the archer and pinned the monster's neck to a tree. Chuckling to herself, Ena surveyed the dead Reptear; maybe twenty of them and she couldn't find any more skulking about. Destruction and death sounded by the hunter's lodge. If Ena had been inside, she would've been able to protect them. Maybe they deserved this.

"Ena, what's going on?" Sal had rushed out the inn like his present would turn the tide in a fight.

"Nothing but Reptear, go back to sleep."

Drawing on the earth and wind, she rushed forward faster than horses. Carnage came into view like she was falling down to the danger. Leben were fighting for their lives with their little spears and bows, but they kind of looked like children at play for all the good they were doing. The Reptear had gotten three Lumber Wockeys to come out and play.

Lumber Wockeys had been one of Narla's favorites. They rarely saw the forest dwelling monsters on their job as Brokers. The monsters were about eight feet tall and made like beetles with a head and neck that could rise up another twenty feet.

Their fronts were held up by six solid arms that ended in three short clawed fingers, equidistant on their gnashing mouth-palms. What made Lumber Wockeys the most threatening were their razor thin whiskers that lashed around their mouths. With a single shake of their head, they could tear apart shields and armor before grabbing a preferred prey with the brow-arms menacing their face.

Erchritt citizens seemed completely incapable of handling a threat that Visk or Torno alone could disperse. It took twenty of their "big strong men" just to distract one of them. Their women were too busy running or cowering to do anything, and these fools actually preferred that to them learning how to wield a weapon. The other two Lumber Wockeys were ripping homes to tinder as they found their cowering women and gnashed them into a meaty paste. Those women died because these men were too insecure to fight besides them and too haughty to let Ena share a few drinks.

Ena didn't even bother with using a gesture. She held out a hand and severed the neck from the corpulent body with an elaborate spearhead she'd been designing. Geomancy kicked up the body, and she ran through its vulnerable underside with a stab of her spear. These monsters were an inconvenience to her and a life lesson that these fools would never learn.

Two more? Fine. Ena killed one with a boot of solid flame. It popped so perfectly that its guts flew a solid forty feet up. Screaming, the cowardly Leben ran to avoid the ichor even as it broke apart into mottle.

Ending the last Lumber Wockey would've been easy if these incompetent men weren't crowded around trying to play hero. One was so determined to die a hero that the Leben man wrapped his entire body around the razor sharp whiskers. The way these people fought was a joke. Grabbing the last Lumber Wockey's head with pure force, Ena pulled it off the ground. A clawing hand of cold, pierced its innards and squished it. The Leben men below were too slow to even avoid its spewing ichor. If the monster hadn't turned into mottle, it might've killed one of them. Ena couldn't help but laugh at their ineptitude.

One of their hex patterned homes burn from where a toe of the flaming boot had touched it. The "big strong men" rushed over to put out the fire and left her alone. Which was all ofr the best. She wasn't in the mood to watch these fools mourn their wives and children. They seemed to think that's all women were good for; dying. They didn't know how strong their women could be if they only let them grab power.

Fuck Erchritt.

A tiny tinge of guilt stirred at her heart. Directing her attention at the destruction, she pulled at the flames. But they didn't respond. Swaying back and forth, Ena couldn't focus on the fire, let alone her surroundings. Ether drain? From that? Ena was right about this village, it sucked. Whatever burnt down was nothing compared to what would've happened if she hadn't been there. Going back to sleep was fine. She didn't owe them anything.

~ ~ ~

It sounded like a mob had come for Ena's head, but the massive crowd woke her with a polite knock. She felt so out of it from passing out the night before. Her flask was open, its contents emptied out on her pillow and bedsheet. It wasn't anything Ena should feel ashamed of. These people owed her their lives. The fact that they would have to pay anything for the inn was sheer madness, but once coins were in hand, the innkeeps weren't going to give it back.

The mob knocked again. Ena put on her rings and cast haste. It took her a good twenty minutes to rub the blue skin paint on, and another three to toss on her clothes. Twenty-three seconds was hardly any wait at all for them, but she still stunk like Torno's butt. After an appraising sniff of her pits, she decided she might smell worse.

The villagers were talking too fast for her to follow.

Too tired to be sociable, Ena looked to Hultur to translate.

"Apparently, there is a rather large collection of Reptear nearby," he told Ngoltur's Aides. "They claim there is something called a-"

"A balebog," Zukoch said, finishing the thought. His Faulchet wasn't as good as Hultur's but he'd been studying the monsters in Narla's manual. "It is a stationary monster that rots the land. Any who die in its pits are reanimated as skeletons. They say the Reptear are protected by an army of skeletons. An entire city has been destroyed by this one rash of Reptear."

"Wait, we're talking about tens of thousands of people dead because of a single group of Reptear feeding a balebog?" Myrrel asked.

"It sounds like they've made a city, but I'm not sure. Tostadt?"

"They have constructed their own word for it," Hultur informed. "A city of the dead."

Ena held up a map to the gathered masses. "Where?"

The children were muttering, "Ngoltur." So much for her disguise.

Some injured man point at her map. Tostadt was indeed right by a city on her map. By the look of where the trade routes lay, it had never been a point of interest so much as a way station to feed lumber and pelts into the inner workings of the Country Without a King. Tostadt was not on their way to Schlabaum and would cost them a three day detour at the least.

"It's too far away," Ena told the group, showing where it lay on the map.

"You're just going to tell them, no?" Torno asked.

She shrugged. "That's how it would've been if we never came along. Whatever government they have must be amassing an army to take care of this."

"That is not the case," Hultur told her. "Erchritt has no standing army."

"What do you mean it has no army? All countries have an army!"

"All public service is done voluntarily. The people of

Erchritt see military quests as a form of public service. Normally when there is a conflict, they would gather all available bodies and rally them together to fight Reptear or whatever threatens to approach."

"Fieta has not conquered them because Karzak is in the way," Visk put together.

"It preserves their old ways," Zukoch told her. "Once all of Leben Erde was ruled like Erchritt, but Hultur's campaigns have brought savagery to Leben Erde. Ngoltur preserves Erchritt to preserve the Leben."

"All the more reason not to help," said Ena. "The Grand Dream has been hampering progress throughout the world. These people need to change. How many Ngolturs rebuilt their failing infrastructure when she could've taught them destruction mage? They're on their own, as they need to be."

They looked at Ena like she'd said something cruel. Sometimes the truth was cruel. That didn't mean it was Ena's fault. She was just pointing out the reality of their overly idealistic country.

"Um..." Zukoch muttered.

"Out with it."

"Normally, balebogs would be destroyed by Muttur. Remember that Reptear were not created by Leben magicians, but by visiting royalty from Gulambar. They had hoped to save the land and instead created a problem that even they couldn't stop. Ngoltur's own granddaughter brought about the lizard-people that ravage these lands. With the cycle of the Grand Dream broken, no one will come to stop threats like this."

"So you're saying because Gulambar messed with the divine order of things, it's now my responsibility to take care of this?" Ena asked.

He gave a non-committal tilt, but Ena was pretty sure where he stood. The others had similar opinions. Myrrel looked like she was between yelling at her and leaving the group. Ena hoped she did leave. They should all leave.

"Tell them I'm not Ngoltur and that we can't help," Ena

told Zukoch.

"What?!"

She rolled her eyes and went to what looked like their village's elder. "Too many bad," Ena told him. "I'm sorry."

They were scowling and gaping at her decision. Hultur was fine with it, but then again, he would be.

"Gather your things. I don't wanna linger here," Ena told her Aides.

They shuffled their feet but did as they were asked. Myrrel in particular seemed livid with her. She had to be the primary instigator of the coup. This drama should put everything into perspective. They weren't here to save Leben Erde from the Reptear. They were on a mission to kill Muttur and end the Grand Dream. They didn't have time to destroy a city of the dead, it was just that simple.

Thankfully, the crowd dispersed. No one was trying to manipulate Ena into solving all the problems of their country. They'd have to wait for their ineffective government to gather something like an army and take care of this themselves. Maybe they could hire some Fieta mercenary companies or something. None of this was Ena's responsibility.

"I have to say that I'm impressed," said Hultur. He was riding beside her on Gale. That horse was supposed to be hers, but without Li'at, Gale was the only one large enough for him. "I feared that their talk of a ruined city would sway you into wasting our time."

"Every day we waste time and there's little we can do about it. An entire city of skeletons is proof that their government is flawed," Ena scoffed.

"Are you willing to take any suggestions?"

"I'm willing to hear them."

"The next time Reptear attack, do not involve yourself. Those people may still suspect that you are Ngoltur with or without your help. If the Brokers handle the monsters they will do nothing too unbelievable."

"They're not Brokers."

"You understood my point as it was made," he said, with a harrumph.

Hultur's comment irked her, but he was right. Ena was taking pointless risks because she was used to thinking like a Broker. Worse than that, she was being carelss by using her full power to destroy the Reptear with haste. She went out with her blue skin covering and now they knew who she was. Torno, Myrrel, Visk, and Sal had destroyed hundreds of monsters without her help. Ena couldn't be responsible for everyone's lives.

THE FORTY-SIXTH CHAPTER

In Which Ena Moves On

There was a great temptation for Ena to forego the day's meeting. They were going to challenge her authority. She knew it was coming. Some part of her itched to have it out. As the sun cast longer shadows, she found herself rolling her casting rings to rub the skin down painful. Sal had found an abandoned house not too far from the main road to "discuss a few things." Ena was having trouble sensing where things were with all of the roots; they gave her too much information when using geomancy to feel. What appeared to be an empty house was a home for a family of cats. The calicos and tuxedos avoided the people setting up a fire in the living room, but they came out to soak in the heat. There was no more avoiding it. The meeting was here at last.

"I'm supporting Hultur's position," Sal said to start the discussion. "I liked things better when we had a wagon. Rolling alongside all of you gives me a better sense of what's around us, but it's lonely."

"Who else wants a wagon?" Ena asked.

Torno, Zukoch, Hultur, and Myrrel all added their hands to Sal's.

"Alright. I guess it can't be helped." Ena sighed, steadying herself for what was coming. "Anything else?"

Eyes met eyes, but none had the courage to speak up. None even looked like they wanted to. They were somber and ready to get whatever sleep they could find. A juvenile tuxedo cat rubbed himself against Ena's arm. She pet the incessant thing. Instead of settling, he twisted around to make Ena pet her how he wished.

"I know you're all probably disappointed with me," Ena said, staring at the cat. "But time isn't on our side. Muttur had at least two relics. One of those relics was the Winged Boots. He'll be able to beat us to most of the ancient treasuries even after we get the relic map from the Grand Dreamer. Beyond that, he seems to have some control of time magic. While I still think that he only uses it to move back through time, it does mean that fighting him on neutral ground will favor Muttur."

None of that was new information. They'd all talked about this so many times. Ena looked up to find the same tired faces.

"I can't speak for everyone, Ena, but I'm not disappointed. This is a shitty situation to be in. I don't think there is a right choice. There's definitely not an easy path ahead." Myrrel was petting a calico matriarch while two juveniles aggressively pushed to get a favored position on her lap.

Ena looked at each of them. They had nothing to say about her not destroying the city of the dead.

"Are you going to use that time rug tonight?" Visk asked.

"Umm..." She took another look around the ruined hut. There wasn't a great place to set up, there were too many holes in the walls. "I don't think I will."

"Then sleep well." Visk poured herself a cup of wine and drank.

There was a lot of drinking and very little talking that night. They had more to say about the cats than Ena's new callous attitude.

Ena dreamt about the Cannegurin girl slowly eating her alive. She couldn't move her body, but she could feel the girl's teeth puncturing her skin. She woke up to a cat chewing on her finger between demanding licks. The faint blue in the sky told Ena it was too late for her to go back to sleep, and too early to start the trip. She went outside and found Visk on watch.

"There's a dead village down that road." Visk pointed into the woods.

"Any signs of what did them in?"

"No bodies and no graves. Maybe Reptear."

Ena nodded.

"There is a statue to Muttur here. Zukoch said it was devoted to him saving the people here some four hundred years ago," she said conversationally.

"Please don't tell me Zukoch was standing watch."

Visk scoffed. "Hardly. The boy couldn't sleep."

"I can relieve you. I'm not tired."

Visk made her way back to the house, grabbing some logs on the way in. They were all so silent. None of them had anything to say to each other. Ena wish they would, even if they were going to yell at her. It was better than this loneliness.

~ ~ ~

There was no talk of Ngoltur in the small town of Aulsa Shaud, but there was a rumor floating around that Muttur was in Doronel. As fast as he was, there was no way he could be in Gulambar. Even if he was, there hadn't been enough time for the news of his arrival to travel back over the ocean. It was strange that people believed Muttur was on the other side of the world, and Ena couldn't make sense of it.

Drinking alone at the bar, Ena hoped her disguise would get her some attention, but no one caught her eye. Some came over to ask what she was drinking and a few lingered long enough to ask her a few questions about why she was traveling, but none attempted a real conversation. Ena figured it had been her poor command of the language, but she was beginning to think that these men just weren't interested in a plain dressed Leben girl.

After her futile trip to the bar on the other side of town, she spotted Torno coming out of an apartment complex. He was smoking and had his jacket draped about his shoulder with the swagger of victory. Ena fell into step beside him. He offered the smoke and she tried it. It was softer than the cigar had been, but it didn't feel like much of anything.

"Was your latest conquest worth the effort?" she asked.

He chuckled. "Is that all you think I do, run around fucking people?"

"Did you?"

Soft peals of laughter died in his throat. "He was too drunk."

"Torno actually has standards," Ena observed. "I'd be impressed if I still cared about what you did with your penis."

"It doesn't look like you're doing a walk of shame yourself. The people of Leben Erde not living up to *your* high standards?" There was more than mockery in the question.

"They're either too weak to be yoked or too strong to be meek." Ena shrugged. "I don't think I like their clothes, either. Leben men dress their profession. They seem to think any excessive flash of color would make them feminine. Do you mind if I probe you with a question?"

"I won't stop you."

"What's up with you and men?" she asked. "When we were working as Brokers, I don't think I ever saw a guy give you a second look."

"We were working in villages," he explained. "The smaller the communities, the more people are all about marriage and building families. Besides, I never got involved with any of those women either."

He was actually talking about this. Ena's heart felt the smallest shiver of life again. "Too afraid of settling down?"

"On the contrary, I was consumed with the thought." He gave her a pointed look.

"And now you're not," she observed, taking what she decided was her last drag.

"And now I'm not."

"So...why the men?" Ena passed over the smoke.

Torno laughed. "Why are you hung up on who I get involved with?"

"I don't know. I've just...I've never been with a woman."

"Really?" He gave her one of those annoying Torno looks

that meant way more than he'd ever own up to.

She punched his arm. "This isn't about me right now."

Chuckling, he raised a hand in acquiescence. "Alright, alright." He took a drag and thought about it. There wasn't much of the smoke left. "With women, they're either too soft and loving or I can't keep up with them."

Ena laughed. "The great Torno meets his match in the bedroom?"

"Oh, all the time," he immediately confirmed. "When a woman wants sex, and I mean *really* wants sex, I can't keep going. I'll be crying mercy after the second go, and she's talking about fucking until the sun comes up. It was one of the things Narla and I were always commiserating about."

He'd said her name.

All the levity left his face. What little mirth in her heart died. They were walking side by side like strangers. She didn't care what he had to say about men anymore. The hotel was close, anyway.

"Ena," he said in a weighted tone.

She stopped walking away from him.

"I'm sorry about what I said back in that village." He swayed with nerves. "If you want to use the rug every night, that's your decision. I worry about you. We all do. I think what Myrrel said was right. It isn't easy being a leader. Narla knew that more than me and I think you've had to make harder choices than she ever did."

"Don't say her name."

"What?"

"I don't want to hear her name." She had to pause to swallow back a swell of forbidden emotions. She couldn't think of her.

"Ena..." he placed a hand on her shoulder.

Ena marched to her room. She fumbled with the key, but when she looked back Torno hadn't followed. He was gone. She could be alone with her tears. She froze the tears one by one, flicking them off her face in that old hate filled habit of hers.

She got inside, locked the door, and silenced the room. No one needed to hear her cry. They couldn't know how close she was to breaking down. They needed to believe that she was strong.

~ ~ ~

Ena was happy to be rid of the horse she'd been riding but was aghast when the group refused to sell off Patches. The horse was a constant reminder of her failure as a leader. She was able to keep five horses and still buy a wagon, though, and that meant that she could still ride around on Gale when the want overtook her. The new four-horse wagon was bigger than the kind they'd rode in Caredor, and the jockey box had enough room for the drivers to stand up properly. It was a damn fine wagon, and spirits immediately picked up once they could all ride together. Ena could hear them laughing and playing games from Gale or the jockey box. They'd needed this comfort. The loss of time was worth the gain in morale. It had to be.

Funds were getting low. Even though they still had some gulda, no one would touch the ether charged crystals. Leben Erde barely understood magic and only seemed to use it to care for their animals. Zukoch wasn't getting any better with his combat magic and would lose to all but the weakest ten-year-olds in Caredor. At least he was a good cook and a patient language teacher. Ena couldn't stand studying Faulchet with Hultur, he was merciless with his corrections.

Moods were definitely improved by the wagon. When they came into a proper walled town, talk of a daily meeting were replaced by suggestions to find a decent tavern. Vomdahaus had people enough for three taverns, and Zukoch was enamored with the oddly named Angry Kikaa. Spirits were mediocre, but between Myrrel picking up men to dance and Sal stomping out beats, the whole building came alive. Ena even joined in the dance and sang along to that infectious, but terrible, Schistrau's Song.

Tossed around the room from hand to hand, she hadn't

known that Torno was in the mix. They came to touch hands and gave each other an apologetic smile. He joined in the singing and Ena got over the embarrassment of them sharing a dance, if even for a few moments. He was smiling again. The warmth of that smile always pulled her in. He made her forget about her past as a child of shame or a canvas for cruel students to leave their mark. That smile was why she kept letting him hold her hand and fall in love with her all over again. That smile was why she always struggled to push him from her mind. When she was passed to the next man, she felt disappointment slide in where elation had started to take shape.

Three more songs and the mood had changed. People were playing cards, drinking, and talking in excited tones about the rumors they'd heard about Ngoltur touring Karzak. Ena slunk over to the bar. For a silver, the bartender agreed to fill up her bull flask with whiskey. She wouldn't have any trouble settling down to her night's retreat on the rug.

"Evening, Little Flower," said Visk. Even when Ena was on a high seat, the woman still towered over her.

"Hey. You having a good time?"

"It isn't as lively as a Ki'an dance, but their hearts are in the right place." Tough as she sounded, she was sweating too. "I love to watch you dance with vigor! Too bad about the skin paint, huh?"

"Oh," Ena got up to leave, but Visk put a hand on her shoulder.

"Those who have noticed have already seen it. I do not think the people of Erchritt like to gossip as much as those in Karzak."

Ena chuckled. "Are you kidding me? They're always talking about some battle in Fieta or the riots in Caredor."

"Those are matters from far away. We will be safe."

"How can you be so sure without speaking the language?"

"Do you not feel the magic in the air? These people shake hands with a grip of empathy. They know we wish to be here in secret, I think."

Ena closed her eyes and felt around the room. She was right. Magic was all over the tavern. It flew between friends and even from patron to servers. Every exchange was marked with a grip of ether. Was that why none of the men were interested in her, because she wasn't touching them with empathy magic?

"You hadn't noticed?" Visk was surprised.

"No. Who told you about this?"

"Myrrel first brought it to my attention. Yeldo's manipulations attuned her to the behavior, I think." Visk refused a bartender's inquiry. "I did not mean to talk about this. I apologize if it upset you."

"I'm alright. What's been on your mind?" Ena asked.

"Torno. Have you warmed up to him at last?"

Ena glanced back at him dancing with Myrrel, laughter doubling her over in his arms. "No. I just think that we're finally coming to an understanding. It's good for us to be friends. It's good for the group."

Visk stared with doubt.

"Hello ladies." Zukoch was so flush parts of him were purple.

Ena ordered another beer.

Visk chuckled at the sight of him. "I think you have danced your last dance."

"Oh, yeah. I'm done. I'm so past done. Ena, do you think you and Visk could help me out?" he asked between panting.

Ena got a fresh mug and glanced back at Zukoch. His embarrassed glances shot to the back where a group of women were giggling. They were about Zukoch and Ena's age, though some of them could be younger by three years. A few of them were looking their way, one of them guarding her eyes like the light of the sun shone from Zukoch. They were flush from dancing.

"You see that vision of beauty over there with her friends, the one wiping her face with a handkerchief?" Zukoch asked.

Visk and Ena shared a knowing smile.

"I really like her, but she's over there with her friends. I think it would be easier if the two of you went with me to talk to her." He made a show of not looking at her.

"Leave this to me and Ena." Visk pat his back. She looked to Ena and motioned for the women. Visk made her way to a table with two men and a dozen empty mugs.

Ena accepted her task to talk to the ladies. She emptied her lungs and felt for the use of magic. When she got close, strands of empathy didn't so much slap her as they pressed against her. The motion of it was almost like the lick of a tongue, but it wasn't unsettling and wet. Ena didn't know how to return the magical gesture.

"Hello, women," Ena said in her most congenial Faulchet. "Can I take this friend?"

The woman was round, full of dimples, and dressed more for fieldwork than romance. Flushed as she was from dancing, her friends pushing her into Ena's hand brought out those rare bits of purple on her cheeks and exposed upper chest. She was laughing all the while, as empathic strands slid up and down Ena's body. Ena did her best to hold onto feelings of confidence and happiness, but her lack of empathy magic was irking her.

Visk had cleared the table and was already leading Zukoch back by the hand. Visk and Ena held back the chairs of the two lovers. They sat and both struggled to meet the other in the eyes.

"Speak with heart," Ena told the woman.

Visk dropped off two towels for the lovers and a server came by with a pitcher of water. The older woman grinned mischievous at the Leben local. They could be related for how her eyes lingered.

Visk and Ena watched the two of them begin their conversation with awkward formalities. Torno, Myrrel, and even Sal had come over to stand beside them.

"How's our champ doing?" asked Torno.

"He is ready to fight, I think," Visk said with a grin.

"They're so cute together," Myrrel cooed. "It reminds me of Delimira and Alred. You remember the two of them?"

"Alred had the extra pinky," Sal recalled. "Their twins were so fat and full of life."

"Remember how mad Ena got when Torno told us that we were going to get them together?" Myrrel asked.

"I wasn't mad," she scoffed.

They hissed with doubt.

"I wasn't! I just thought he was pushing Alred too hard."

"I believe your exact words were, 'You are a sad ugly man so unloveable that you have to force others to have what you never can.' You also froze my cigarette." Torno recalled to fits of laughter.

"Narla, do you remember how you..." Ena looked over and of course she wasn't there. Mirth disappeared again; like it had never been there at all. She needed to run from the tears.

Myrrel held her tight.

Ena hugged her, and cried onto her big soft shoulder.

~ ~ ~

The former Brokers retired to Ena's room. They stayed up late, drinking as they reminisced about Narla. Each had a favorite story of their time with her, and for the memories they shared, new details were added by others who'd seen her before or after the incident. It evoked a lot of tears, laughs, and hugs. Torno was the first to leave the conversation by passing out on the floor. Visk left shortly after he started snoring, insisting that she needed to get some sleep. But Myrrel and Sal stayed behind, soaking up the opportunity to share their early days with Narla. They'd served with her for almost seven years.

"Myr." Ena slurred her words affectionately. "Why don't you want me to lead?"

"I do."

"You don't."

They drunkenly went back and forth like that for a time.

"Ena," Sal spoke up.

"Huh?"

"Why do you think Myrrel doesn't want you to lead?"

"Cause...I'm bad. I'm a bad person. I got Narla killed," Ena said, calm as every other thing a wasted person could get out.

"Camellia, you can't...don't talk like that," Myrrel grumbled. She mashed her face into Ena's cheek. "You can't blame yourself!"

"I can do whatever I want, I'm the fucking Wise Ruler!" Ena flung her body back and half fell off the bed.

Sal helped her onto the floor. "Then save the people. Shouldn't we be doing good while we're on our quest? Isn't that why Hultur isn't in charge?"

"Hultur isn't in charge because..." Ena sniffed. "You know why! Myr, you heard him right?" She didn't answer. Ena had to pick her head up and put her chin on the bed. "Myr. Myrrel?"

She was close to sobbing again, but she'd cried too much to do it again. "You didn't use the rug last night, did you?"

Ena tried to shake her head, but the bed made that impossible. "How did...Sal, how did Myrrel know that?"

"She's smart." He reached around for his jug of oil and found only a few drops inside. He licked them off his fingers.

"I hate that rug," Myrrel said.

"I hate it too," Ena confessed. "I hate being alone in that fucking circle. I hate that the only way for me to get powerful is to ignore everything. It's...I don't like it!"

Torno popped his head off the floor. His eyes were wide and bloodshot. "Burn it!"

Ea smacked him. "Don't scare me!"

"Burn it," he repeated. "Myrrel, help me get her to burn it."

"Torno, just tell her to do the opposite," Myrrel laughed.

Sal laughed along with her. "Yeah, she hate doing what you say, Torno!"

"Do it, Ena. Jump back in the circle," Torno said with a slurred voice and a sloppy grin on his spineless body.

"I'm..." Ena crawled over and grabbed his head by his hair and his cheek. "I'm in charge now. You can't tell me to do nothing!"

Swallowing, the man could back up and grew rouge with

confusion. "I can, because...because..."

They leaned forward for an explanation.

"Because I'm drunk," he laughed. He laughed so hard that he fell onto the floor again.

"Fine," Ena agreed. "All drunk requests will be fulfilled."

She crawled under the bed of the inn and pulled out the rug. Ena slapped it onto Sal's lap. Swaying back and forth, she picked herself off the floor and sat up. "Everyone say it with me now!" She recited a basic incantation of fire, one of the first learned by any child in Gulambar. When she finished, Ena clapped to incinerate the rug. It didn't spread over the floor. It didn't catch the bed. It just went up in a blaze to coat Sal with bib of soot.

Ena felt sober enough to feel sick and she felt awake enough to be consumed by a tight, constricting feeling in her chest. She fell into Sal's arms. The rocks of his body weren't even hot.

"Sal, I'm sorry I'm touching your balls," she said in all seriousness.

"Not a problem. I got balls of stone," he said without levity.

Ena didn't remember falling asleep. She didn't remember dreaming. She didn't remember crawling around the floor of the inn. So it was a little weird when she woke up next to Torno's feet. She'd been cradling them like two little kittens in her sleep and her mouth tasted like sweat, feet, and acidic bile when she woke.

"Torno?" Ena asked, but he didn't answer. He was actually asleep. She slid around the floor to look at his scruffy face.

Torno was drooling on a very unmagical rug. So much of it was caught up in his beard and it smelled like turned booze besides, but the sight of him on the floor stilled her. Torno was defenseless. Ena could do anything to him. She could poke him in the eyes and make him blind. That thought comforted her. He trusted her enough to sleep on the floor with her. He was on this horrible journey too. He'd left his entire life behind, but he was never sad about his family.

Ena fell asleep looking at his ugly face.

~ ~ ~

Morning came too early. Sure, Myrrel had magic to lessen the effects of being hung over, but there was no spell to cure sleeplessness. Ena wanted nothing to do with morning and less to do with being awake. She remembered most of the night before, the most dramatic of it had been burning that fucking rug. It was best not to dwell on that. Drunk Ena had made a decision that sober Ena had to live with.

Zukoch looked pretty sleepy himself when he got out of his room at the inn. Everyone watched him obliviously working the ropes of the wagon. Ena buzzed around him like he was a fresh spring flower and her the bee.

"I had a great time," he said with a chuckle.

"An unforgettable time?" Visk asked.

"The kind of time that you won't forget for as long as you live?" Torno asked.

Ena giggled and then leaned in to whisper into his ear. "Did you fuck?"

He blushed indigo but didn't smile. "You know, some find it rude to share the intimate details of their lives."

"Those people must live really interesting lives," Myrrel pouted. "Me? These Leben men aren't biting..."

"Company," Sal warned.

Zukoch's little girlfriend from the night before was there with a few friends. Some of them had bags. Little Miss Dimples walked up to say "hi" to the group.

"Everyone, this is Kludel," Zukoch said, introducing her. He repeated it again in Faulchet.

"Hello. You are all beautiful spirits," Kludel said in Faulchet. "Were you traveling to Schlabaum?"

Hultur translated and all eyes were on Zukoch for an entirely different reason.

"I told her where we were going and nothing else."

After a bit of back and forth, they came to learn that Kludel and her three friends were interested in traveling with them to Schlabaum. They'd been planning a trip to the city for some time but the threat of Reptear kept them in town. Between the four of them, they had two Schistrau and a cattle-drawn cart. The Schistrau might slow them down a little, but the cart would cut their travel time in half.

"I'm sorry," Zukoch told Kludel. "We have a tight schedule to keep."

"It's alright," Ena told the lovers. "You can ride with her in the cart and we'll take one of you with us in the wagon."

"Your heart's swayed at last by love?" Sal asked in a friendly tease.

"It's on the way." Ena shrugged. "Besides, I need to modify my haste spell with Hultur."

"You really mean it?" Zukoch asked with a smile. He and his sweetheart were positively glowing.

Torno didn't believe her for one second. "A new haste spell, huh?"

"You big softy," Myrrel whispered.
Ena didn't care about what they said. The two had formed a strong connection in just one night. In two more nights, they'd have more time together than Ena had to say goodbye to Haenir. Besides, if Zukoch had a really great time, maybe he'd leave them for good. Ena hoped he would.

THE FORTY-SEVENTH CHAPTER

When the Meet the Grand Dreamer

Geometry and math were too esoteric to sap Ena's focus away from the horrors of the Chantry, but she usually understood. The fact that she needed this knowledge to construct time magic spheroids spoke volumes about how far high magic had shifted from raw creation. Visk could perform imbuing with dance moves, and Ena had to solve math problems and construct a glyph one piece at a time to adjust the time bubble to the shape and speed she wanted. Still, when she cast the haste spell over the entire cattle-drawn cart, it filled her with pride. She'd done it on her own. She figured it out without Hultur's help.

Better yet, Zukoch had twice as much time to bask in the sun and spend time with Kludel. If Ena could cast a love spell, she would have. Though they hardly needed her help. Every time she looked their way, they were either kissing or staring into each other's eyes and talking about nothing and everything. Ena spent enough time gawking at them for Visk to chide on her for being creepy.

The other Leben newcomers were interesting. Ena had originally mistaken the man and woman on the schistrau as a couple, but Anior and Grou were just friends and apparently not even good ones. Nineteen-year-old Anior had left his village to find a man to love. He was a competent jeweler by birth but was ready to take whatever job he could find. Anior had a romantic encounter with a gem cutter from Schlabaum last winter and was hoping to reconnect with him.

Grou was the seventeen-year-old daughter of dairy farmer and she left to get away from sister's husband. The man was a lecher. Not content to merely cheat on his wife with his mother-in-law, he was making passes at Grou. Her mother sounded like the overbearing type and all of her focus was on turning Grou into the perfect wife. The only man who had shown her any interest had been this hog farmer she described as greasier than the bacon he sold.

They heard most of this from Bogelb, who rode in the wagon with them. She'd learned how to be a hunter with the help of her widowed uncle. Despite her skill with the bow and ability to track prey two days gone, Bogelb had been denied membership to her village's Hunter's Lodge based solely on her gender. They'd come up with any reason but that, but last summer the woman of twenty-one had been passed over for an unskilled boy of fifteen. She'd learned Dorospek from her late aunt-in-law and brother-in-law and spoke with a southern dialect that made her sound like the villagers Ena used to work with.

Among them, only Kludel didn't have a reason for leaving her village. As far as Bogelb could tell, she had gone on this trip just to have more time with Zukoch. Bogelb hadn't been shy about sharing her fears about their relationship. The eighteen-year-old Kludel's only experience with love had been a secret crush she'd held onto for four years and that ended with the man marrying Kludel's older sister. Small village drama being what it was, she still had to see the man daily.

It was all very dramatic and very familiar to Ena. Small villages were full of crushes that lasted years and grudges that survived generations. Most couldn't even conceive of leaving, but these four were taking a chance on the future. Ena enjoyed listening to Bogelb and her endless stories about their small village drama and so when the great tree of Schlabaum came into view, Ena found herself wanting to slow down.

They'd finally come out of the woods, and small villages were sown together like patches on a quilt surrounding the great city. Other patches were a mixture of farmlands and grazing plots, that stretched out from the edge of the woods all the way to the heart of Schlabaum. According to Bogelb, they were already in Schlabaum, but this was definitely the city outskirts, and it had been one of the largest Ena had ever seen. After trading a fresh cow to replace the tired heifer, Grou said goodbye to the young lady starting her own life. Zukoch and Kludel were in deep sleep under a blanket, haste having made it late night for their bodies. If anything else happened...Well, everyone kept their eyes forward and the wagon stayed at least three minutes ahead of the cart.

It was still night when they arrived in Schlabaum's northernmost district, marked by the end of farmlands, and the beginning of apartments. In a show of surprising generosity, Bogelb paid for their lodging and Anior bought them drinks. Ena tried to talk to the lovequesting Anior, but he had a thick Karzak accent and even Schlabaum natives had a hard time understanding him. Visk tried to show the lanky man how to dance, and lead him through something Visk called, "the dance of feathers."

The entire tavern became enraptured by Visk's display, and she somehow got everyone to attempt the dance without speaking a word of Faulchet. When the band decided to play the one Ki'an song they knew it ended with three black eyes, five fat lips, and twenty stubbed toes. Myrrel kept laughing as more injured came to receive her services. Ena focused on the dance itself trying to feel how Ki'an dance could command ether.

Near halfway through the next day's travel, they reach the canopy of the mawnah tree. It was time for Bogelb, Anior, Grou, and Kludel to split. Zukoch and Visk volunteered to help the four get their bearings in the vast city. Visk and Bogleb went with Anior to find the gem cutter and Zukoch went to help Grou sell her cow and find jobs and lodging for the four of them. It was ambitious, but Zukoch knew his way around the cities of Leben Erde.

Ngoltur and her Aids said their goodbyes and went to

meet the Grand Dreamer.

While no Mawnah could be described as anything but majestic, Schlabaum's drew in the eye. The bark of the tree was black, and everywhere the bark had been stripped away, red flesh met the eye. Its leaves were almost completely gold and blinding to gaze upon directly.

Even drowsy and drunk, Ena felt the heart of the tree beating. Ether didn't rain down in a drizzle like it had in Taulge, instead it flowed from the canopy in an endless stream. Ethereal power was thicken than water in the streets. Any standing under the Mawnah could cast all day with that power coursing through them. Not only did Hultur feel it but so did Torno and Myrrel. This tree was putting out thousands of gulda worth of ether and no one in the city gave it a second thought.

A twenty-foot-tall yellow wooden wall surround the base of the Mawnah. The fortifications were a work of pure artistry with a painted mural connecting each hexagonal watchtower. The murals honored Muttur, they mourned those lost to Hultur's invasions, and thanked the world for this age of peace. People wandered in and out of the gate, with many buying trinkets of the Turall. Travelers from one edge of the world to the other were there to see the Tree that Bleeds, the Wall of Destiny, and the glorious inner city that kept the same architectural style for fourteen hundred years.

Entering the northern gate was a daunting task of pushing past bodies. Three forty foot tall statues ignored the tree to stare at each other with greed, wrath, and desperation. Hultur, Muttur, and Ngoltur stood in the center of a hexagonal fountain large enough to be public pool. Yet the crowd wasn't there just to gaze at the statues of gold, adamantium, and mythril. Their eyes were on a bare plinth where three Dreamers waited.

"What's going on?" Ena asked Hultur.

"The Dreamers rarely leave the inner palace and when they do, the three do not come together."

"Part!" shouted the Green Dreamer.

The two Dreamers echoed the first and their Disciples pushed at the crowd. Waves of empathy magic poured off these religious leaders. Even flowing through the crowd, Ena still felt a need to silence and bow her head. It triggered memories of being brought before the Wizard who stationed her in Caredor.

"I do not like this," Myrrel growled.

"Just think about the Supreme Magus," said Torno resolute. "It keeps my head exactly where I want it."

Ena held onto the memory Courage, the Green Dreamer in Taulge that had no answers for her. That silenced all her feelings of reverence.

The three Dreamers approached Ena. "Please follow us," said the Dreamer in blue. "The Grand Dreamer is waiting for you."

Ena looked to Hultur. "Did you send a letter to them?"

"No, this is legitimately impressive."

"The Dreamers control the city," Torno reminded them. "They probably identified us the second we bought our hotel room."

"I'm still finding it hard to focus my thoughts," Sal admitted.

Ena fell into step beside Sal, her shoulder against his cheek. "Relax. They should cool with the empathy bombs once we're past the crowds."

"But the crowds are following us."

They were. And with the knowledge that all three Dreamers were outside, all eyes were jumping right to Hultur.

"Was this what you were looking for?" Ena asked Hultur. "Fame and prestige?"

"After the pathetic encounter we had in Taulge, I'll content myself to raid their library."

The inner walls of the innermost part of the city were left bare inside. Unlike so many panels and posts, not a line of script lay on the yellow walls. But they were buzzing with ethereal power. Red human-sized crystals at the top of the gate were lightly tapped by archers and they shifted blue. Passing through the gate, another tap brought the crystals back to red and a solid wall of black kept the tourists from following. It wasn't a wall of force, but pure ether. This was old world power, magic from the first Ngoltur.

Hultur was practically drooling. "That gate! I must study it!"

"Eyes forward," Ena told him. "They've held onto the secret to that magic for three thousand years."

"There is no secret to it," said Wisdom, the Blue Dreamer. They sounded much older than the one Ena had met in Taulge. "It uses the magic of the Red Mawnah. It cannot be reproduced anywhere. There was a Doronel scholar who studied it not fifty years ago. If you wish to learn more of the gate, you will need to find her book. Secrets Before Time, I think she named it. I'm afraid the Grand Dreamer has too much to discuss to be delayed."

Hultur nodded and followed along.

They were led into a courtyard garden. For all the majesty of the tourist haven outside, it was a garden as simple as any villager's. The flowers were native but well cultivated. Floorboards and walls were left raw and unenchanted. Kneeling before a sprig of lavender was a short woman in pure white robes. Her skin was a blue softer than the noon sky and her hair was dyed white-tinted flaxen.

The Disciples waited outside the garden's humble entrance with Power holding open the door. Wisdom waved them forward, making sure all had come inside. The three Dreamers knelt before the leben woman at the garden, touching their foreheads to the ground.

"Grand Dreamer," said Courage. "They have arrived."

She pulled the lavender plant out by the roots and stood.

The Grand Dreamer was a woman that defied explanation. Her beauty was simultaneously gush-inducing cute and full of awe-inspiring grace. Round maternal sex appeal spoke of a fertility proven but lithe limbs lacked a mother's strength. Skin the softest glacial blue suggested she spent a life indoors, but these were hands that lived with effort. No more was her conflicting life laid bare than the contrast of adorable vibrant round cheeks support a beleaguered gaze that held the responsibility of the world in her eyes. Even those wise, captivating irises were the green of freshly grown flowers at the darn of spring surrounded by veins of hard gemstone. She had the look of a woman who had seen the world three times over and known the turmoil of the poorest beggar, the richest Queen. Ena's heart quickened to meet her eyes.

The Grand Dreamer smiled gently, knowingly and with sympathetic lust. "Hello, Ena. We will have our time together as soon as I can. May I?" She knelt before Ena and took her hand.

It felt wrong. Ena was supposed to be kneeling for her. She could only watch with words trapped in her throat as she brought the back of Ena's hand to her lips. Those lips were so tender and soft. Ena's skin shocked electric to feel the smooth touch of this Leben woman. Her eyes gazed past her bowed head and into the loose garments of her thin robe of white. Under it, Ena saw the shape of her breast and the very edge of her areola. Lust and shame battled in her mind, and lust remained victorious as it took in this gorgeous woman slowly rising back to her feet.

Ena was sweating.

The Grand Dreamer placed the lavender in Ena's hand. "Forgive me, Wise Ruler, for I have only this simple gift to honor your arrival."

"I am beneath the honor it bestows," Ena said out of a habit she'd never learned. The words felt natural, but her mind struggled to place when she'd ever even heard them. She looked away from those soft eyes and that comely body to view the plant. It was nothing more than a simple stem of lavender, but it brought tears she could not explain.

"Hultur, I will talk to you first. Courage, please bring Ngoltur and her Aides to the baths. Power, when they are done please bring Ngoltur to me." She turned about giving Ena a sensual view of the curves of her behind and the firm rigidity of her legs.

"Wait, isn't anyone going to talk to us?" Torno asked of the Grand Dreamer.

She looked back and gave him a coy smile. "Oh, Torno. You aren't ready to handle the truths we would tell you. But if it will satisfy your curiosity, Wisdom will parlay with you in the study after your bath. Everything else, I'm afraid you'll have to keep waiting for."

"Waiting for what?" Torno asked, not following her.

"Satisfaction," said the Grand Dreamer. She led Hultur deeper into the palace by his finger.

Courage offered to take the lavender and led them into another part of the palace. Though elaborate on the outside, the interior was just as simple as the garden had been. It was a place of modest comforts. Along one wall, paintings of various levels of skill lay unmounted and unframed. On the other, pottery and woven baskets sat.

"These are our works of art," Courage informed them. "Each of us had a hand in the work that decorate our home."

Ena found herself drawn to a flower blooming out of a snowflake. Most of the paper was white, save the black flames around the edge of the paper. The paint had warped the shape of the paper, and the color of the red flower and blueish snowflake were already starting to fade.

"That is the Grand Dreamer's. You have good tastes, young Ngoltur." Courage paused to decline her head. "If you'll follow me, I will lead you all to the baths."

Ena had thought they were using baths in some kind of colloquial term, but each of them were shown to a private bath. No Disciples were left behind to care for Ena. The boudoir had a chaise lounge, closet, and a standing vanity. Behind one door was a shower to scrub down and a tiled floor that led to a heated bath. On the vanity was a letter. It smelled of lavender and turmeric.

> *Ena*
> *I know these luxuries unsettle you, but it was my wish to*

welcome you with kindness. Please indulge in them as if none are present. Though it is forward of me to say this, I advise you to burn off your shorthairs. You may come to regret it otherwise.

Sylene

Sylene? Was that the Grand Dreamer's name? The Dreamers had no names. And what was that about shorthairs? Had she seen how Ena's eyes had trailed over her body? Maybe she was working lust magic on her. Though such things weren't supposed to be possible Caredor had obviously been keeping a great many things from their people. Ena decided not to trust Sylene.

While Ena was washing off the blue, she did burn off her pubic hairs, but just because they were getting a little long. She'd been planning to do it anyway, once she had a proper shower. It had nothing to do with that woman's beautiful tits or kissable lips. Whatever spells of seduction she'd woven, Ena felt no residue of their power on her. No magic flowed to heat the water either. But there was some kind of oil mixed into it. The liquid smelled like green tea and washed over her body like cream.

Three outfits waited for her in the boudoir.

One, the same simple robe of sheer white that Sylene wore. Ena was not about to walk out to greet her friends wearing something that would probably show off her nipples.

The other was a Caredor gown taken right from the closet of the Great Generation. No, it was more than just any gown. It was the same red and blue number that Kalta had worn in her romantic escape, the same that Torno had slid off her chocolate skin before burying his face into her smooth pussy. Magic or not, the memories of that dress sliding off brought a flush of life to Ena cheeks.

The final outfit was a set of traveler's clothes very close to the kind Ena wore when Hultur met her. This one, of course, shouldn't have the missing button, but it was gone. It had the same red threads from where Narla had sown a back strap back on. The outfit was the same, except Ena had gotten rid of that back in...well, back when she was with Haenir. She'd worn it when she lost her virginity. That is, she wore it shortly before losing her virginity.

Sylene was fucking with her.

Another note lay in the pocket.

> *Ena*
>
> *Hopefully by now I have proven that I am no mere charlatan. I have known you for all my life. I am not here to trick you to play the game of the Gods. I only wish that you will take me as I am. If I could, I would be everything that you wanted but I can only be myself.*
>
> *These garments represent sexual beginnings for you. It is my hope that we can begin things not only with lust but also love. There is so much love in that heart of yours, I only ask that you listen to it. I know it is still hurting and it will hurt more before your journey is over. But I have been chosen to help you. Please listen to me before you have dismissed what I have to teach you.*
>
> *Sylene*

This was only getting weirder. If she was trying to win her over by being so forward, Ena didn't see how it would work. Then again, with a body like hers, she had probably never been turned down in her life. Ena could teach her rejection if she kept her wits about her. There was a temptation to just put on her old traveler's clothes and get the fuck out of there. But then she wouldn't get the map of the relics and she wouldn't learn whatever this seductress meant to teach her.

Back and forth, her eyes went from the white robe to the traveler's clothes. Ena bit her lip as she struggled to pick.

THE FORTY-EIGHTH CHAPTER

Where Ena Learns About Empathy

Rebellion spurred Ena to dress in a mixture of Kalta's dress and the traveling clothes. From the waist down it was trousers and boots, but the skirt of Kalta's red gown exposed one leg of the skin tight gray trousers. The parts of her skin that would naturally be exposed by the plunging neckline of the gown were instead covered by the white button-up of her travel-wear. She repurposed a blue belt into a scarf. Her hair was still too short to do much with it, but she worked an asymmetrical thin braid over the left. For makeup she went naturalistic, the kind she'd worn while serving as a Broker.

Power looked twice when Ena came out to have herself escorted to meet this temptress. They were staring at Ena's exposed leg, until she let out a little cough. Power righted their posture and led the way forward.

The route to Selene avoided Ena's friends and was planned with such precision that she passed through seven rooms and walkways in the palace proper without seeing another soul. It was only her and Power until they reached the garden. A Disciple waited by the entrance with the lavender in hand. The Gulam woman wouldn't meet her eyes and could've been a dresser.

"Do you want to bring the lavender?" Power asked.

Ena had forgotten all about the lavender, but as her eyes hung on the plant she was filled with nostalgia and a growing sense of mourning. "The time for this has passed." Again, familiar words found her, but she didn't know where they came from. Ena couldn't escape the feeling that she'd said this before.

Past the simple garden a small receiving room opened to a private domicile. Ena added her boots to a shoe rack filled with common footwear and took in the modest bookshelves and cleaning supplies organized against the walls.

"Will you wait here?" asked Power. Ena agreed and they left her.

Snooping a little, Ena found a closet with a note stuck on shin-high table. It read, "Please set this up and wait for me to finish." Ena frowned. She'd done what Sylene expected again. Instead, Ena checked the door on the other side of the room. There was a small kitchenette with ether-powered devices that could be found in apartments all over Caredor City, a refrigerator, an electric oven with connected stove, and a crystal operated sink. She'd seen a kitchenette like this before. Not exactly like this, there was more clutter before. There was a faint smell of oolong tea.

Hultur sniffed loudly. He barely fit in the small room and was forced to bow his head while inside. His perennially red cheeks were wet from tears. He wasn't wearing his glasses and there was no sign that he'd ever owned a hat. Power left his side to set up the table.

Ena stepped closer but found Hultur unwelcoming. "Are you alright?"

He was slow to respond and barely shook his head at all. "She is what we've been searching for." He swallowed back fear and met Ena's eyes. "Do not waste time asking her to prove her claims."

"Alright." Ena risked a hand on his arm.

He flinched at the touch. When he sighed to steady himself, the ceiling creaked from where his shoulders rolled against the wood. "I will need some time to process what I have been told."

"Are you ready to leave, Vamere?" Power asked.

Ena scowled at the use of the fake name, but Hultur nodded with acquiescence and followed. He barely fit through the door.

Three drinks sat on the table: ale in a tall glass mug, steaming tea in a fancy cup and saucer, and pink juice resting in a bright yellow fruit cut open. Ena sat down and examined the cup of tea in the middle. It was old enough to have the delicate golden script worn down by use. She recognized the script as old Dorospek, though she couldn't speak a word of it. Tempted to drink, she couldn't get that saucer up to her lips with that fruit in her eyeline. Ena was pretty sure it was a mango, but that wasn't mango juice inside. She tried it and found the juice pleasant and smooth, like a peach or apple without a hint of anything tart.

Sylene chuckled behind her.

She was standing on the threshold in that damnable sheer robe. Crouched as Ena was, the woman's crotch was more or less at eye level. She could see a darkness there where the legs came together. The folds of the drapery hugged the mound of her belly and pressed out where her breasts hung. The shape and color of her areolas were an undeniable purple. Looking away from her flesh took an effort and came with nowhere near enough shame.

Sylene was full of mirth. "Oh, I love what you've put on."

"You didn't give me much to work with," Ena grumbled.

Sylene entered the room and picked up the ale and tea. "Would you mind opening the door to the outside?"

Ena did.

The woman slipped into raised wooden sandals and handed the drinks over to a Disciple, before coming back. There was a smile on her lips that never went away. She pulled back a hunk of that gorgeous white and flaxen hair and basked in the sun's warmth. Ena hadn't moved from the edge of the screen and her ass brushed up against Ena's hips as she returned.

"Do you want to keep your juice?" Sylene asked gently. When she shook her head, Sylene put it in her kitchenette and then came back to put the table away. She waited by the entrance to the inner chamber. No, it was her bedroom they'd be going to. Ena was sure of that. There was nowhere else she'd be going with this gorgeous woman.

Ena closed her eyes and focused. "I want you to stop using lust magic on me."

"I would never do that to you, Ena. I promise you. Everything you're feeling for me is coming from you. If you'd like, I can put something on to hide my figure, but I'd prefer that I didn't." Her voice was a spring breeze drifting through the leaves of a tall, shady tree.

"Why can't we be civil?" Ena asked more aggressively than she meant to.

Sylene looked down bashfully before the splendor of her eyes focused on Ena. "Because I like how you look at me."

Ena swallowed. There was so much heat in that look. If Sylene asked her to, she'd rip off her clothes. She liked how Sylene returned that look. There was so much more than lust in those eyes. All of this giddiness and flirtation came because Sylene liked her.

"Maybe you should cover up," Ena grumbled.

"As you wish. Feel free to follow me into my room."

Ena didn't. She waited in that receiving room for something to happen. Like, for example, if her heart slowed down, that would be great. Ena had been attracted to women before, but never like this. Before, Ena had wanted to watch a woman flit about a room or soak in the happiness of a kiss they shared. This time, Ena wanted to be the woman she kissed. She wanted to feel Sylene's lips again, only she didn't want things to stop at a greeting. Ena needed to stop thinking about this woman's body. She was here for answers about the Turall, not to have sex!

Sylene came out in an off-yellow sweater that hugged her chest. From the waist down, a toned leg peaked out of a thrice-cut pleated skirt. It was two simple articles of clothing, but they hid so little. Ena didn't want her to hide. She wanted to run her hands over those legs and feel the softness of that sweater while she moaned for more.

Ena looked away. "Is that really the most modest thing you

could've worn?!"

"No," Sylene admitted. "But I did rather not waste a lot of time getting dressed."

The implication was clear and Ena's pounding heart agreed wholeheartedly.

Sylene walked into the hall and motioned to her bedroom door. The study was on the other side. Two clothes resting on a shin-high table, one had been used and the other was folded into a tetrahedron.

Ena bullied her way into the study crouching before the folded cloth. Sylene closed the door behind them. Shamelessly she stared at Ena's chest. The dress shirt showed very little of Ena's body, but one of the buttons was strained taut by her flesh.

"Why are you doing this?" Ena grumbled. "Why are you seducing me?"

"I can't help how I feel about you, and I have far less power over what you feel about me." Her voice came out in sultry tones. It would sound so much better if they were fucking.

Ena tried to shut everything out and feel the magic in the air. But she could only feel the endless flow of the Red Mawnah pouring over them. If Ena paid very close attention to the flow of ether, she could feel a pulse from the tree. It was the same pulse that was swelling through Ena's body and slowly working blood into her clit.

"Listen!" Ena slammed her hands onto the desk. "I have a lot of questions and this isn't helping."

"I understand that, Ena, but you've made it very clear that you don't want me to anticipate your questions." She held her hands out in apology.

"I never said anything like that."

"You did in my dreams." Sylene chuckled nervously and lowered her eyes. "I've been dreaming about today, for a long *long* time."

"You're a Sage," Ena put together.

Sylene nodded. "I'm one of the strongest they've ever seen. The Dreamers taught me how to control my dreams and through them I've been able to gaze into the future and learn things about your past."

"You know what's going to happen." Ena excitement was cut down by a realization. "You knew what was going to happen! You knew Narla was going to die and you didn't warn me!"

Sylene bowed her head. "There was no easy way to send word to you. I am also watched over by the Gods, and they do not want me interfering."

"That's bullshit! You should've tried!"

"I did," she said slowly. "I tried to run away to Gulambar when I was seventeen, and I was blocked at every turn. By the time I reached the edge of Erchritt, the Dreamers had caught up with me. They warned that fate couldn't be changed by their actions, but I still tried to send word to you. All of my letters were intercepted or destroyed before they ever crossed the ocean. Besides, I had been seeing a different future."

"Wait, one thing at a time," Ena growled. "You said that you tried to come see me when you were seventeen. How old are you?"

"I share your same birthday, Ena. So you are now a little older than me; I think by about five months."

"How does that make any sense?" Ena remembered the circle. "The rug of haste."

Sylene bowed her head gently. "Tempted as I was to share that pain, the Dreamers could not find anyone capable of doing what you and Vamere accomplished."

"Why are you calling him Vamere? And what do you mean you saw a different future?" Ena closed her eyes. "I asked you not to say too much!"

"I'm sorry, Ena. There's so much you don't know. It makes it hard for me to explain everything without confusing you. Please know that I am trying. This is very scary for me." Her hands were shaking. She placed them on her thighs to hide them under the table.

"You're scared?" Ena couldn't believe what she was hearing.

"I really like you," she confessed. Sylene tilted her head up and let out a stabilizing breath.

Ena had to look away to not give into that urge to hug her and tell her that everything would be okay. "Please answer my questions."

"I am calling Hultur Vamere because I asked him to reconsider using the name of a conqueror and he agreed. Vamere asked me not to tell you more." Sylene paused to see if Ena would push the issue.

"What about this business with a different future?"

"Peering into the future is never precise. It is easy to slip from one future into another without knowing that's what occurred. It is why so many Sages are confused by the visions they receive. When the Grand Dream is stable and the players all play their part, everything is well behaved and the Sages can find each other with perfect precision. But you and Vamere are both acting with chaos. You are driven not by fate, but by your hearts and minds. As such, every major decision changes fate in dramatic ways."

Ena considered how damning this information was, but pushed on. "What did you see to make you try to come to me three years ago?"

"I was asked not to tell you that, but I am not compelled to."

She'd break that covenant if Ena made her. Ena knew she should drop the issue there, but curiosity made her lean in. She could smell the lavender and turmeric of this woman's musk. It was really distracting to share this room meant for one. "Who, um, who asked you to keep things from me?"

"Ena, I want to kiss you."

Ena bit her lip. "You barely know me."

That wasn't exactly true. This woman had apparently dreamt about her for years. Sylene didn't say anything. Her hands were shifting about, but Ena didn't dare see the look of lust on her face or the squirming of her body.

"Please answer my question," Ena demanded.

"Vamere did not want you to know about some of my dreams of the future."

That meant that the outcome of Sylene's worst dream involved Hultur. If she was trying to cross the ocean to get to her, that had to mean the negative future involved Vamere. Sylene seemed to care a great deal about her. She used the word "love" in her letter. Love wasn't something that strangers were supposed to feel for each other. But something about how Sylene looked at her made Ena believe that she did feel that way. Hadn't Ena loved Torno before ever meeting him?

"Ena, it will be easier to talk after I teach you." That fucking sultry voice again.

"What...what are you going to teach me?" It was so hard for Ena to catch her breath.

This woman *was* a seductress. Just the smell of her made Ena's heart flutter. Ena risked a glance at the woman. She looked pained to wait so long to touch Ena and the sight of Ena's eyes brought a smile of relief. Her soft sky-blue skin was almost lavender from the blush rushing over her. Sylene tried to keep her eyes on hers, but they wandered over her neck, or fixated on some part on her arm, or the shape of her shoulder and breasts.

Sylene swallowed. "You need to learn empathy magic to succeed. We have books that you could read, but you don't have the time. I can show you with exercises, but those would take weeks. If I teach you in the first way, you will understand in moments."

"What's the first way?"

"The people of Leben Erde learned empathy magic through the meeting of spirit, mind, and body. There is only one thing in life that is such a perfect merging of two that empathy comes without thinking." Sylene couldn't keep her lips together, her breath was so labored.

Ena knew what Sylene was talking about but it sounded absurd. The empathy magic that kept a land in peace was learned from sex? In Caredor, empathy magic had charts of glyphs, tables of effects, and thoughts that resonated with different kinds of animals. The two cultures approaches to magic couldn't be more different if Ena spent years trying to construct a new one from scratch.

Sylene was obviously willing to teach her with her body and that body was so enticing. The sweater did a poor job of hiding its curves. A bead of sweat was rolling down the side of her neck. Her lips were wet from a compulsion for Sylene to lick or bite them. A frosted haze glimmered her eyes as the focused on Ena. She wanted to kiss her. She wanted to touch her. The magic was an excuse, and Ena found herself caring very little about magic.

"How would we begin?" Ena whispered.

"You'd follow me to my bedroom and get undressed."

"Then?"

"I'd undress."

"And?"

"It's easier to show you."

Ena wanted to see that naked body. She'd seen her shape under that sheer robe, but the sight of her bare skin had to be better. It had been over a month in normal time since Obi pounded her. He'd been so large and forceful, the pain of him had to come with the pleasure. With Sylene, would there be any pain? Maybe Ena could have as much pain as she craved. Empathy magic would mean that Sylene felt everything Ena was feeling. She could satisfy her desires as soon as they came.

Standing, Sylene held out a hand. She looked nervous again, scared for things that she'd known from other encounters. "Come with me."

"How do I know I won't lose myself to your magic?" she asked timidly.

"You will," Sylene promised with a smile. "And so will I. We will step outside of ourselves and become us. If you fear it, that fear will become you, but if you accept the loss of control, then we will share a glorious orgasm."

Fuck. How could Ena say no to that?

She took Sylene's hand and rose to her feet. Soft hands

steadied her rise. They caressed her shoulders and applied a longing pressure as they slid down her bicep. Her lips were so close now. They beckoned Ena to press into her and know the feel of those lips. Sylene took her hands between them and smiled with building excitement. Leading Ena into the bedroom, Sylene sat on the bed and crossed her legs tight – wincing from the need she felt.

Ena needed to start by undressing.

First came the scarf. It was never meant to be a scarf and tickled her skin as it slid over her neck. She pulled off the gown. A flash of Torno's lips kissing the moist mound of her pelvis. She undid the buttons. Haenir's lips had found her neck and his hands rubbed the flesh of her ass. She slid the undershirt up. He'd rubbed at her ribs and kneaded at her belly. Her belly was so taught now, firm from days of eating practically nothing as she tortured herself in that circle.

"Eyes on me," Sylene said.

She'd sensed it. She'd sense Ena straying without sending out a single strand of ether. Those dazzling eyes saw everything. She knew what Ena had been through, knew dark thoughts that Ena had been too scared to tell herself.

Sylene told her, "From the first moment I saw you I wanted to kiss you. I can't believe you would share this moment with me. I feel unworthy of your touch."

"But you're gorgeous. You could have anyone you want."

"I only want you," Sylene confessed. "In the world of flesh none have touched me, but I'm not scared. I love your pink skin, Ena. I want to see more of it."

Ena slid a playful finger under her brassiere. "Are you sure you can handle it?"

"I know I can't," she giggled. She reached up and didn't just rub her breast, but gave it a squeeze. "I want to lose myself to you."

That was definitely encouraging. Ena ran her hand over her own breast, teasing it gently with her palm. Her erect nipple jolted from the sensation of soft fabric. Sylene's nipples were hard with arousal, pressing against the shape of that sexy sweater. Ena worked off her belt. Sylene squirmed to watch Ena run her fingers under the hem of her trousers. Her legs came out fast, born of a habit of never having to undress to please.

Sylene let out an audible whimper. Hungry eyes stared at Ena's crotch. She wanted her so bad. Ena tilted her hips to hide the lips of her pussy and she whimpered again. One foot on the bed, she slid off the trousers and brought her bare skin into view.

"Oh, fuck..." Sylene whimpered. She crossed her legs the other way. She pinched at her nipple. "It wasn't supposed to happen like this."

"Do I surprise you?" Ena teased.

"Every time."

Ena snapped, burning off her brassiere and panties in a single flash of controlled fire. Sylene had been a beacon of sexual desire for Ena, but it had been Ena who was in control. This woman was salivating to be with her. She could barely take a single breath without needing to swallow. There wasn't a single part of Ena that she didn't desire, and the poor woman looked pained to try and control her lust or even just to find a favored part of Ena to stare at.

Ena leaned forward.

Sylene responded in kind, craning her head forward to meet Ena's lips.

A single soft hand on her cheek held back her eager lips. Leaning in, she whispered, "Your turn."

Sylene pained to wait for her. "You're so sexy, Ena."

"I know," she said, the smile dominating her expression.

Sylene stood up and steadied herself with a sigh. "I can do this."

Sylene pulled her arms into her sweater. Tilting this way and that, she found the cutest side of her face and kept it there to stare at Ena. Those arms came up to expose smooth skin. Her breasts were plump from excitement and dominated her chest; nipples swollen to purple. Her soft, smooth hair danced over the curves of her shoulders and Sylene pulled it back and forth, letting the yellow tinge platinum strand dance over her front.

Pressing those athletic legs together, it only took a flick for her to push the skirt off. Her red panties were black at the crotch. Wet to the point of being fragrant, Ena stepped up to savor her. She smelled like honeyed meat, and fuck if she didn't look juicy. A self-conscious hand ran over the roundness of her belly and fingered her stretch marks. Sylene lost the battle to keep her face serious and on the woman she'd waited years to meet.

Ena caressed her cheek. Sylene closed her eyes and leaned into her firm grasp.

"You're supposed to teach me," Ena reminded her with a whisper.

"But you teach me how to be a woman," Sylene gasped. "I can barely breathe."

Ena put her hands on her ribs. "These need to expand."

They started filling up before she even said the words.

"And now you let it out. It's okay if you let out little moans," Ena encouraged.

Sylene bit her lip. "Whimper or a moan?"

Ena ran her hand over the hem of her panties. She'd meant to tease her a little longer, but the round flesh of her belly brought Ena's fingers down. Those legs parted obediently. Her hips tilted up to receive her. She quivered as fingers went from dry fabric, to damp, and finally came to rest on her wetness. The woman was soaked, the fabric barely an afterthought on her person. Ena could feel the shape of her swollen clit pressing out. She rubbed the base of it gently, probing her for one spot that might feel better than another.

Sylene whimpered. She gripped Ena's arm with claws. She could barely stand.

"Moan," Ena whispered into her ear.

She did.

The sound of that full, deep voice sure turned the tables on her. One moment Ena had been completely in control of what was happening and the next she could barely keep her eyes open. She smelled like honey, turmeric, and sex. Her skin was soft and salty against Ena's lips. She hadn't remembered leaning her head against her shoulder, but was happy to kiss as those gorgeous moans rumbled through her chest.

Sylene pulled back to slid out of her panties. A wet trail clung to her inner thigh. They were naked before each other and Sylene was so fucking ready for what was coming. But she was holding back still. She raised her hand for a demonstration.

Ena took her wrist.

She startled but stayed still. "What about the magic?"

"Do it."

There was some kind of protest vibrating her throat, but Ena silenced her with a kiss. She melted into Ena's firm embrace. Ena brought her leg up between her knees. A squeak came out and then that rumbling moan returned, and Sylene hit her with magic. The part of her brain that processed magic felt it not as a strand, but as a fabric full and warm as Sylene's skin. Every grinding push against Sylene's crotch tickled Ena's own clit. Then tactile sensations went out the fucking door.

Playful desire had motivated Ena, but she wasn't playing around. This fuck was her life. There was nothing but Ena. The feel of her mouth was perfect in life, a kiss that confirmed every good sensation she'd ever known. Just her tongue was enough for Sylene to fall back on the bed and ooze into a pile of happiness. Moaning was the only conscious thought rolling through her head. She had to remember to moan, to keep Ena as happy as Ena made her. Her heart felt less like a machine and more like the ocean. It rolled on with warmth and filled her with purpose. She had purpose now. She could make Ena happy. She knew she could.

They were on the bed. Ena pulled back from the kiss as the caress of ether left her. Sylene was still kissing, smacking her lips against her neck. Ena had lost her breath now. She had been Sylene for a moment, felt everything as if she was her. It was intense. This woman felt more for her than Ena had felt for any person in her life. She didn't just want to fuck her she wanted their hearts to join. Sylene's hand rolled down Ena's taught belly.

"Your turn," she whispered between kisses.

"I don't know how…" There was the fear. It was building.

"Feel my fingers. Hear the deep rumble of my aroused voice. Know that I can come again."

"You…Just like that?" Ena asked with excitement.

Sylene kissed her and pulled back to smile. "It's only going to get better. Let me in."

Ena parted her legs.

Her fingers teased around her flesh. "Into your heart."

"How…?"

Sylene kissed her. She thought it was a preamble to more explanations, but then Ena stopped caring about the magic. Warmth was in that kiss. It said so much about how Sylene felt about her. Ena needed to push back. She pushed with her tongue and tilted her hips. Responding, the smooth roll of her ecstasy flickered like embers given wind.

Sex felt good. Ena liked it. She liked this woman. She wanted to feel her breasts. She wanted to force out those moans from rolling orgasms. She grabbed at her breasts and squeezed. She sucked at her neck and pressed her teeth against the skin. That moan came back. That fucking moan robbed her of her senses. It made her push into those skillful fingers, rocking back and forth as her body shook involuntarily.

Ena was wincing now. She could barely breathe. She was suffocated by pleasure and an oppressive push of magic. She pushed back, grabbing her shoulders as she forced ether out. She was stronger than the tree. She was a force of power and she needed this woman to keep working her fingers into her. She needed to feel that strong push of pleasure take her. She came with a scream. It didn't stop. Orgasm gripped her body. She shook, burned, and screamed all over again.

Breast were by her face. Ena sucked at them, licking and grabbing to show her appreciation.

"Oh, fuck, Ena," Sylene panted. "That was so strong. You're so strong."

"More," Ena growled, her face half buried in her nipple. "I

want more. Show me everything."

Sylene had waited her whole life to teach Ena, and now it was time for her to get to work. Ena hoped she'd be up to the task. Something primal had opened in Ena and she wasn't content to stop. She wanted to fuck every part of this woman, she wanted to overwhelm her. She grabbed Sylene's legs, forced them apart, and kissed. When that empathy hit Ena, she felt every flick of her tongue. She'd never licked so fast in her entire fucking life.

This was going to be a long lesson.

THE FORTY-NINTH CHAPTER

In Which Ena is Shown Lies

Evocation was shaping magic into whatever form the caster desired. By contrast, empathy magic was like pushing out raw ether at people. The magic of Gulambar was like speaking with letters on a page but the craft practiced in Leben Erde was closer to communicating with grunts and shouts. While limited in nuance, it was actually more effective at getting to the heart of what was trying to be communicated. Much like bleeding, Leben magic required Ena to abandon all she's learned from the Chantry. It required her to act without a conscious framework and to respond to incoming information in the same way. Since sex had a way of shutting off conscious thought anyway, Ena was able to respond to the magic intuitively. Soon, she was able to feel Sylene at the same time she was sharing, and what should've become a sexual feedback loop instead expedited the two toward an indeniable truth.

This wasn't going to work between them.

Sylene loved her. She'd devoted her entire life to Ena. As sweet as that might be, it wasn't what Ena wanted from her or any woman. They realized it in a shared instant. Sylene was taken by the pain of it. She threw herself into Ena's shoulder and cried. She'd known it was coming, but since reality was never certain Sylene had held onto hope. Knowing that Ena couldn't return those feelings hurt.

They were dressed in sheer white robes and eating a squash stew in Sylene's receiving room. It was full of smoke and pepper flavor and surprisingly filling for something without meat. Ena felt bad about what she'd done to this woman, but some tender idealism curbed her guilt. How could it be wrong to use someone when that person wanted to be used? Somehow Ena knew Torno would have the answer.

"Visk warned me about this," Ena told Sylene. "She said that if I just wanted to fool around with Torno then I'd hurt him."

"Is that what you want from Torno?"

Ena focused on her stew. "Are you really sure you want to talk about me and other people?"

"Absolutely," she said with conviction. "Ena, I love you. All I want is for you to find happiness. You're not happy. You seem to think that you can't be happy because you're Ngoltur, but you're not."

"I'm not what?"

"You're not Ngoltur."

Ena dropped her spoon. Feelings of doubt radiated out with her magic but contained the cloy sweet of hope.

Sylene spoke with the same confidence that she did about anything that wasn't her feelings towards Ena. "Do you remember when you were served the three drinks when you came in? Those drinks represent the Three Prime Gods, the ones that choose the Turall. The Dreamers came up with those drinks because they seemed to be what the Turall preferred to drink. Can I take your meal?"

Ena nodded.

She took the squash rinds and continued to talk as she put them away. "Thoughtful Tea for Ngoltur, Brutal Beer for Hultur, and Joyful Juice for Muttur. Originally, the Dreamers thought these preferences came about because of their ages. Hultur was typically five to ten years older than Ngoltur, and the same between her and Muttur."

"Wait, Ngoltur is always about five years older than Muttur?"

Sylene handed Ena a mug and a cold bottle of beer. "Why do you think Ngoltur is never interested in marrying him? He's usually thirteen to fifteen when he saves Ngoltur. Only once in the history of the Grand Dream was he ever seventeen, and then he was bound to turn into a wolf every time there was a full moon. It was an odd dream."

Ena poured the beer into the mug.

Sylene came back with a cup in the shape of an apple on a plain saucer. She placed the two out on the table. "Think of these as the blessings the Gods historically given the Turall."

"Oh, I thought you were getting me a beer. I didn't realize they were for a demonstration."

"No, I want a beer too."

Ena sipped at the beer and then offered it to Sylene.

Sylene took a quick sip and then placed it on the vertex of an unseen equilateral triangle. "Hultur downs the beer and is filled with power. Ngoltur sips the tea and receives wisdom. Muttur drinks his juice and knows courage."

"Those don't seem balanced," said Ena.

"They are balanced by contrast and need. Each is more than just three drinks or three parts of the psyche. These three represent fundamental differences in reality. We could also look at them as the past, present, and future; birth, growth, and death; mind, body, and spirit; and so on. Each of these in isolation can be broken apart, but even two of them together are more than enough to overwhelm the third. If any single person were to ever drink from all three, they would have the power of the Gods."

Sylene took a sip from the beer.

Ena smirked and pointed at the suds on her lip.

Sylene was taken by sorrow again but leaned back to focus on the three cups. "Anyway, when I gave this test to Hultur, he went for the tea." She slid the tea over to where the beer was. "And you tried the juice." She moved the juice to where the tea had been.

Ena drank two full gulps from the beer and placed it down on the empty spot where the juice had been. "So people are trading drinks?"

"I think the Gods are. We've never thought of them as being these drinks, merely that they like to drink them. If you think of them as three friends sitting down at a table like this, they've traded. Vamere was supposed to drink from his mug of ale, but he reached across and drank from the tea. He pursued knowledge. You were then forced to sip from courage, and now Muttur is obsessed with power."

"You're telling me that I don't have knowledge? That I'm not the Wise Ruler?"

"You have knowledge, but it is not divine wisdom. There is a difference. You are not Ngoltur. Spiritually, you are closer to Muttur. You are the brave hero who must stop senseless destruction." Sylene finished off the mug. With her explanation finished, that somberness rolled over her.

Ena felt bad for her, but she wasn't sure what she could say to cheer her up. "I'm sorry I don't love you."

Sylene smiled but shook her head. "Please don't apologize for that. I've known this was coming," she said again. "I will come out of this heartbreak stronger for it. I worry that the same won't happen for you."

"I don't find love?" Ena got two more beers from the fridge.

"Usually not," Sylene confirmed. "But this unfolding of events has been substantially different. You could be married and pregnant by the time this Grand Dream comes to an end. I do not know with certainty what is coming, but I can say that the road ahead will not be easy."

Ena handed Sylene her own bottle. "Someone I know is going to die."

"Yes. I'm sorry."

Ena looked at the empty mug. There were still some suds inside, the bubbles popping away.

"To new beginnings?" Sylene asked, offering the bottle.

Ena clicked it and they drank.

"I'd come with you if I could, but every time I do I die a predetermined death and in very little time."

"What do you mean by a predetermined death?"

"We're riding fast into the woods and a branch pokes my eye and kills me. I sleep by a campfire and a branch falls spreading the fire to my sleeping bag."

"Are your deaths usually tree related?" Ena tried to joke.

Sylene looked up at the Red Mawnah. "Yes."

"How is it that you can even see the future? How do you know about Torno and Zukoch and all of my Aides?"

"Dream magic. The Dreamers can control their dreams, even divine dreams. So when I dreamt of you arriving here, I could control what we did and use that to meet your friends and move on to try and help you on your quest," she explained.

"And we usually have sex."

"Every time." Sylene took a drink. "I've tried to keep that from happening, but you always find me and...I can't tell you no."

"Is that why you came out in this see through robe?" Ena gestured at the too revealing outfit.

Sylene nodded. "I wanted to try seducing you. I almost kept it up this time."

"You did."

They shared a drink.

"How long have you been dreaming about us?" Ena asked.

"Since I've been born. The dreams didn't become sexual until the night you saw Torno's Romantic Escape with Kalta. My sexual awakening was timed with yours. The Gods want me to serve you and I'm done trying to deny it. I've tried running away, but I can't stop thinking about you."

"You can now," Ena assured her. "You've given me knowledge of empathy magic, you've told me that I'm not Ngoltur, so now you can move on, right?"

Sylene bowed her head. "We have to meet again."

"I'm coming back?"

"Once more. When you ignore my words and try to set a trap to kill Muttur, he kills you. You are tempted to jump to the conclusion that you and Vamere can overpower Muttur, but you are wrong. I don't know how he is so powerful, but I suspect it is because he has been favored by Brutal Beer."

"Why do you keep calling him Muttur?" Ena asked. "If I'm not Ngoltur and Vamere's not Hultur, then he wouldn't be Muttur, right?"

"That's absolutely true, but I've never learned his name. Traveling up to this point in time has been easy, but I have only moved forward to our second meeting ten times."

"Can you tell me what's coming?"

"I could, but it will change the outcome. For all I know, I've already changed what is meant to come. I will say that this is another convergence, a moment of great choice. You will either go straight to Vytur Castle to get Magoloiherdir or you will stay in Leben Erde to get as many relics as you can before Muttur can."

Ena's head was spinning again. There was too much to assess, too many risks to measure. This woman was a wealth of information and it was already past sunset. If she stayed much longer, she'd have to sleep there. Ena didn't want to worsen this woman's pain by sleeping with her again. It was easier to focus on prophecy than to think about how she'd wronged her.

"The, uh, sword. What happens if Muttur gets it?"

"He destroys Vytur Castle and kills parliament. When you and Vamere finally catch up with him, he kills you. He unites the Harminelds, conquers Ki'an, and then goes on to bring the entire world under his power. If Muttur gets Magoloiherdir, he becomes unstoppable."

"Fuck. No pressure, right?"

Sylene gave a grim nod.

Ena stood up. "Where is the map with the relics?"

"Torno will have it. You aren't going to stay the night." She stood. Sylene didn't ask what Ena's intentions were, she simply accept what Ena felt.

"I think it would be wrong to stay."

"I wouldn't resent it, Ena. I cherish every moment I have with you. Even though you've closed your heart off to love, you still have so much to offer. I still want you to kiss me. I want to kiss you."

Ena didn't like the sound of that. "What do you mean I've closed off my heart to love? I'm because I don't want to use you. I fucked up by having sex with you, I'll admit that, but that doesn't mean I'm incapable of love."

"Of course you're not incapable of it. But Ena, you will not let it into your heart right now."

"I loved Haenir. I may have left him, but after that night I loved him still. I want nothing but the best for him."

"You were a different person then, Ena." She sounded so fucking sure of herself.

"Shut up! I don't like how you're talking. You don't know me! You knew them, you knew the other me, but not this one. I surprise you each time. You said that yourself! Stop using your experiences in other timelines to influence what happens in this one!" Ena stomped back into the bedroom to find her traveling clothes. She was getting sick of this woman.

"Ena, we didn't just have sex. I felt you. I felt your intentions from the deepest core of yourself. You have closed yourself off to the idea of love. Why do you think I'm so sad? Do you think all I care about is you staying to be with me? You can't even talk about *it*." She said, "it," but something about the word was weighted. There was something Sylene wasn't saying and it had to be from the other timelines, despite what she was insisting.

"I can talk about love." Ena was halfway through getting changed. She could leave soon. "I'm talking about love right now and I'm telling you that I want it. I just don't have the luxury to kill time really getting to know people. My body craves sex and my mind craves intimacy. I'm not a monster for hooking up with people if everyone involved knows what's happening. You knew what this was about. You could've stopped me at any time. Don't get mad at me for your mistake!"

"Ena, you're the only one who is mad." Sylene could easily fake her calm delivery.

"You're trying to tell me that you're not mad that I fucked you and now I'm leaving? I saw you when you realized that we could never be! I saw how much it hurt you to know that I only wanted sex from you." Ena walked out into the receiving room. "Where are my boots?"

Sylene pointed to the shoe rack. "I wasn't crying for my pain, but yours. This is the risk with empathy magic. You can know what someone is feeling, but you never truly know the reasons. Some believe that even we can't know the reasons for what we feel."

"Those people are dumb. And don't change the subject! I've had too much of that in my life. People always change the subject when they don't want to hear hard truths."

Sylene suppressed a guffaw too late.

"Did you just laugh at me?!" Ena finished tying her boots and stood.

"I'm sorry." She waved her hands.

"What, did we rip my shirt or something?"

"Ena, you're accusing me of what you're doing," Sylene said, sweet as she could. She was trying to mollify her anger.

Fuck that. Ena wanted to be angry. There was plenty to be angry about. "You don't know me. You don't know what I've been through, despite what the other versions of me have told you. What we've had is all that we've had, and you don't know what's going on in my head!"

She was wearing a smirk worse than any Torno had ever put on.

"Whatever you think you know, just say it." Ena got up in her face. "Say it. Or are you too afraid to live in the here and now? You dreamed about me, but that's not me. I like you. I liked our time together, but I don't like you talking to me like you know more about me than I know myself. Stop being a coward and tell me what you think I can't handle."

"You can't talk about Torno," she said simply.

Ena laughed. It came out so suddenly that she laughed in her face. "I'm sorry." She chuckled some more. "Is that what this is about? You're jealous of Torno?"

"If we're being honest, I don't like how you ignore my

thoughts. I've told you so many times that I am not sad because we can't be together. I knew that was coming before you even arrived."

"You're sad because I've closed off my heart."

"Yes."

"That's bullshit! I haven't closed off my heart." Ena slid back the door to the garden. She finally put together what the Grand Dreamer was trying to get at. The thought held Ena there. It shook up fear in her heart and the more she considered the words, the more that fear grew.

"Ena, please come back inside. I can help you with this as well."

She did close the door, but she didn't step up to the raised floor. "Sylene, I want you to listen to me."

Her change in tone sobered Sylene. She stepped back from her sanctimonious attitude and let herself be vulnerable once again. She was scared, but it was the fear Ena had been living with for months now, half a year when the slowed time was considered. She didn't want to die. She didn't want to live a pointless life.

"Sylene, you can't live for me. As much as you like me, I'm not the world. Even if we were together I wouldn't want that for you. What I did was a mistake. It was sexy and sweaty and satisfying, but it was a mistake. The fact that you let it happen, it breaks my heart. It breaks my heart to think that you...

"Look, I don't know what I feel for Torno, but you obviously think that I love him. Maybe you think that I should marry him and have his children, but you took me into your bedroom. We made love, Sylene. I felt how much that meant to you, and you don't even care that you can't be with me. You should be sad for the life that the Gods have kept you from living. No one should live for another person, Sylene. Even if it's someone you love with everything you are, if they don't love you back, you need to move on."

Sylene was crying. She had to compose herself to ask, "Is that why you told Torno to move on?"

Ena nodded. "I can't be with him. It would be too weird."

Sylene closed her eyes. Tears ran down her cheeks in trails and then they stopped. She let out a short, strong sigh. "I want you to try one last empathy exercise."

"Only if you agree to stop waiting for me." Ena was asking a lot from her. She'd been thinking about Ena her entire life.

Sylene kept her eyes closed and took her time considering that and what it would mean for her. "Okay, I can do that. Now I want you to close your eyes and empty your mind. I'm going to say a word and send your feelings back to you."

~ ~ ~

Torno and Visk were back at the hotel bar. There was a single clarinetist playing a smooth melody. Ena stood by them at the high table. There was an empty third seat that belonged to Bogelb, the hunter denied access to her guild. The Leben woman was in the restroom. Ena ordered a gin and tonic. With any luck, the bitter liquor would keep her from drinking more.

"How did things go?" Ena asked Visk.

"Anior's beau was married. The man would to continue the affair but the truth of his life broke Anior's heart. He's burning away the deepest fats in the heat of his rejection."

"What about you?" Torno asked.

Ena blushed. "This is some powerful music. It really hits you, huh?"

Torno hadn't noticed the music and neither had she. But him listening and reacting gave Ena the chance to settle her nerves.

"Good news is that the Grand Dreamer is the real deal. She knew everything about us and has a fairly accurate idea of what's coming. That's also the bad news. Muttur is almost unstoppable and if he gets Magoloiherdir, that's it. He destroys Vytur Castle and goes on to rule the world."

"Then we get there first," Torno said with confidence.

"What good will it do?" Visk asked. "For thousands of

years Muttur has been the only one to draw Magoloiherdir."

"You got the relic map, Torno?"

"Yeah, but I haven't had time to copy it yet." He rummaged through his bag.

"I can draw the sword, too. It's kind of a long story, and I don't really get it myself, but Sylene thinks I'll be able to pull the sword out of the stone." She took in the general form of the map. "Do we know which relic is in what treasury?"

Torno pointed out the Faulchet words. "I can't read them myself."

Bogelb came back. "Hey. How'd your date with destiny go?"

"Good. Do you know what each of these relics are and what they do?"

Bogelb glanced at the map. "Not at all, sorry. I didn't pay attention to any of that stuff at devotions."

Ena nodded and gave Torno the map. "How's Grou? Did you and her find a place to live?"

"Yeah, Kludel said that Zukoch found her a job in a bazaar. I guess she and Grou will be working side by side. Kludel made it sound like Zukoch was a miracle worker. They're upstairs right now. Probably banging it out. He's a good guy, right?" Bogelb was looking at Ena.

"Zukoch is really sweet and we haven't treated him as well as he deserves. I think he'll be kind to Kludel."

"But he's not going to stay." Spite broke through Bogelb's voice.

"Kludel knows that," Torno reminded her. "Whatever they're doing, she knows it can't be forever."

Bogelb scowled at him and Visk added to the righteous damnation. Ena would've been right there with them a short time ago, but she knew what it was like to be in that situation. Sometimes two people could only love each other for a day, sometimes there was only an hour to work out that attraction. She felt so different about love now. Torno tilted his head when he didn't find Ena's judgmental scowl. Something caught his eye.

Myrrel was walking with worried alacrity. "We need you, Ena."

"Who's hurt?"

"It's Vamere. He's freaking out. Visk, I'll need you and Torno, too. Bogelb, you're a nice woman, but he needs to have people close to him right now."

"Yeah, got it." Bogelb stood to stretch. "I'll go chat with Grou."

The three of them followed Myrrel. Torno spoke first, needing to know what the problem was. Maybe he thought keeping Myrrel talking would help her calm, but Myrrel looked like a wreck.

"What's wrong with the big guy, bad magic calculations?" Torno whispered.

"He has been insisting we call him Vamere," Visk told Ena.

"It's about that, Visk. He's losing it. He's losing his sense of self, and now he's starting to push me and Sal out."

"Why not leave him alone?" Torno stepped into the rotating lift.

Myrrel glanced up at the second floor to make sure none could hear. "Because he still has the power of a Turall. If he loses control, he could burn the entire hotel down."

"No, we're in the torus of the Red Mawnah's power." Ena couldn't think of how to break this news without sending them all into a panic, but this was a threat they couldn't underestimate. "If he loses control, he'll have hundreds of thousands of gulda to draw on. If Vamere starts rage casting, he could kill three and a half million people."

THE FIFTIETH CHAPTER

When Vamere Dies

Chaotic was the academic way to speak of casters who lost control. For the magically weak or inept, a mental breakdown could result in hurting a few people around them. Chaotics drew on intense emotions and had been known to cast intuitively and well above their level. Not all Chaotics surpassed their normal effectiveness. Chaotics with a purpose or a grudge tended to be too grounded in reality to cause any harm worse than a caster going all out. Those who suffered from an identity crisis were a different story. After losing their sense of self, they didn't think about how to cast and seemed to draw on a source of ether outside of themselves. Some believed that Chaotics were driven by the God of Evil itself.

As Brokers, an unspoken part of their job was to remove Chaotics. The official policy on was to kill them outright. Torno had outright rejected that approach. Any time someone was losing control, the Brokers did everything they could to bring them back to civilization and rational thought. But they had seen the devastation one Chaotic could wreak, and they'd had to end the lives of four Chaotics. Every time Torno had insisted that he be the one to end their lives.

As the new leader, Ena would have to make that same decision. She wasn't even sure she could kill Hultur if it came to it. Though he was Vamere now. She needed to remember his name.

All of this had something to do with what Sylene told him. She had to have known this was a risk, but she took it anyway.

Sylene might be able to view alternate timelines, but she was still a woman of twenty. She could make mistakes. Especially, if she was spending all her time thinking about how best to serve Ena. No time to process that guilt, let alone the hard truth Sylene made Ena swallow.

"Where is he?" Ena asked Myrrel.

"I had to move him into my room because he kept talking about burning his books." Myrrel sounded exhausted.

"How long have you been talking to him?" Ena asked.

"A little before sunset, so I guess about three or four hours. I've tried everything I could think of, but he isn't responding. I don't know if he's afraid to open up or if he's unable to. I can't get a read on him."

Torno put his hand on her back. "You've done what you could. We'll take it from here, Myrrel."

"I won't let him hurt anyone." Ena gripped her arm. "I promise."

Myrrel nodded. "I'm gonna sleep on his bed. Don't bring him back here."

Visk gave her a firm hug goodbye. Then they all did.

"Torno, you go in there and relieve Sal." Ena paced as she waited.

Sal left the hotel room exhausted, his face pebbly from a long day. He leaned against the hallway wall. "It's bad, Ena."

"What's wrong with him?"

"It has something to do with his past, but he won't go into it. He keeps talking about these broad philosophical ideas. We spent almost two hours talking about the nature of good and evil only for him to call morality a tool for government to control the masses. I can't tell what's about him and which are concepts bothering him. Myrrel was able to get two things out of him, he's mad at himself for mistakes he's made and something the Grand Dreamer said really fucked him up."

"Okay. Thanks, Sal. You go get some rest."

They punched fists.

"What are you going to tell him?" Visk asked.

"I don't know. Are you going to be okay being in the room?"

"You may need my help," Visk said. "I know the world that he came from, you have not even seen it."

Ena nodded and walked in.

Vamere was on the floor. Pressed up against a corner. There had been a nightstand there, but it and the bed were against a wall. Even crouched, the massive Ki'an was almost at eye level with Ena. There was no sign of his glasses, his hat, his coat, or even his overshirt. The man looked unhinged, his long black hair cast about his shoulders like the roots of a Mawnah. He was clad in an undershirt that clung to his full pectorals. There were no scars on his red body, but intricate tattoos of black ran down his forearm and along his chest. At a glance they looked like glyphs, but they weren't Gulam Glyphs. She'd never seen anything like them, not even in Ki'an cities.

He was talking to Torno when Ena entered. "In that case, you and the others may leave me. I am more than capable of taking my own life, and I would do that before letting my rage take control of my magic again."

"I'm not going to let you kill yourself, Vamere," Ena said to interject herself into this dire conversation.

"Ah, Ena," he chuckled. "Have you come to laugh at my sad state?"

"I've come to talk to a friend."

That unsettling smile spread over his lips. "Come now, Ena. There's no need to lie to me. I am the great destroyer. Hultur reborn. Isn't that why Visk is here with you, to kill me if I ever become a threat? I'm a threat." He raised his chin and pointed to his artery. "I believe the spear point goes here."

"Stop this, Hul-" Ena shook her head. "Vamere, this isn't going to help you. You need to stop thinking of suicide. There are no solutions down that path, only beautiful lies."

"You're not sure what to call me, are you, Ena?" He chuckled. "That's fine. I do not know what to call myself. *Dumu'gi* should suffice. Right, Visk?"

"A daughter who has failed her mother," Visk translated. "You are not that person. You are not what the Geshuri wanted you to be."

"I'm worse." His eyes were far away. He was seeing horrors that snarled his lips. "At least as *Dumu'gi* I wouldn't have hurt anyone."

"You would've lived as a beggar. At best you would've died running supplies for warriors. Neither are deaths the Geshuri would've praised. Have you truly come to accept the wisdom of the Geshuri?" Visk challenged.

His dark eyes took in the wall. He looked bored of the conversation. "You are barely trying," he grumbled. "I can think of better arguments before they even leave your mouth, but I can see why you wouldn't bother. I am not worth the effort."

"Hey, I'm gonna go down and grab me some whiskey," Torno told him in a kind voice. "You want some?"

"I do not drink."

"The old you didn't. New you, new rules, right?" He gave a playful smirk. "How about it? Should I pick up a bottle?"

Vamere considered it for a second but ultimately shook his head. "I can't lose control."

"I'll get some just in case," he said with a smile.

"Bring Nikani," Visk told him. It was a strong Ki'an alcohol famed for its ability to kill flies who hovered above it and sterilize the tools of surgeons.

Vamere seemed to remember Ena was there. "When you were in the private room in Taulge, what did you see?"

Ena cracked a smile. "What does it matter? That place was a joke, right?"

"Sylene suggested that what we saw was what the Gods wanted us to see. I found ignorance and responded with rage, because the Gods wanted me to know that I had not mastered anger any more than I had conquered insecurity. So, I am curious, what did you see?"

"Two people were having sex. They were reprimanded and ran out the room."

Vamere laughed. "Been having an interesting sex life, Ena?" He snorted. "I suppose it's none of my business." He scratched at the wallpaper. "She's one of us, you know? Sylene. She was chosen by the Gods, and now she's fighting to change a system almost three thousand years old. She had to fight to acquire those simple living conditions. They were meant for her private Disciple, and so she switched places with her underling. Now her Disciple is indolent, spending her days waiting outside the garden that Sylene has forbidden any but the Dreamers to enter. It's clever in a way."

"Vamere, I don't want to talk about Sylene or the Grand Dream. I want to talk about you. You chose to be Hultur, right? Why don't you tell me about that?"

His tired head lulled against the wall and he set himself to peeling the wallpaper with four furious fingers. He tore with purpose, following the shape of the wood grain. Some part of it would tear and the wall would follow.

"Vamere, tell me about how you became Hultur."

"I was never Hultur. I picked the name, it was not given to me, so I cannot be Hultur."

"But you stopped being Eres of the Volain clan," Visk said. "When did that happen? How did you stop being Eres?"

He could only shake his head and swallow repeatedly.

"We're here to help you," Ena insisted. "No matter what you tell us, we won't punish you for it."

"Are you really sure you're ready to commit to that?" he asked with a twisted smile. He looked at Visk and cackled. It sounded like the cackle the performers used when they played Hultur on the stage. It was deep, pitiless, and sadistic.

"What have you done?" Visk's fists were clenched.

Off came a long strip, the wall exposed almost to the baseboard. "Got your blood boiling, do I? The great Viskursang of the unbent Lugamud clan has found a reason to fight again?"

Ena got between them. "Visk, I think it might be better if you wait outside." She wasn't looking at Ena. "Visk!"

"He is evil, Ena."

"He is human. We all have reasons to hate ourselves. You're feeding into his self-hatred by acknowledging this. What's going to happen if he decides he is evil? What will that mean for the world? You need to leave."

"Oh, I am evil, little Ena," Vamere cackled. "I am evil by the definitions of all people. It is my birthright."

"Go!" she shouted at Visk, who was still staring him down.

Visk walked back, never taking her eyes off him, and shut the door.

"You're not evil! We aren't what the Gods want us to be. You're supposed to be on my side, remember? We work together to end the Grand Dream. That's the plan. It's still the plan."

"I accepted the rambling of philosophers to justify the crimes I committed, because none could punish me. Even now you couldn't stop me. Powerful as you've become, my physical superiority will be the deciding factor. You will die in my hands." He looked happy to think about ending her.

Ena had to close her eyes. She couldn't give in to the narrative he was spinning. "Some parts of those philosophies appealed to you. They gave you hope, didn't they? Why? Remember what they said."

"They said that morality is a lie, that it is another tool of government. Ethics are always coupled with religion because it allows them to recontextualize all actions of the government as moral and all thoughts of descent as bad. But those were the ramblings of wealthy refugees who had the luxury of whining about a world without reason."

Sal had warned Ena about this, but she was falling into it. This discussion would go nowhere.

"Am I boring you?" he asked.

Ena's eyes snapped open. She steadied her breathing. "I need you to tell me how you stopped being Eres Volain."

He snarled. "You need nothing. You have the world on your side. You were born a hero to be celebrated. I was born to kill."

"Damn it, Vamere! Just fucking answer me!"

"There's that rage. It's never that far away, is it? It's always there, hiding like bed bugs. No matter what you do, they always come back to suck our blood."

"Who did you kill, Vamere?"

His thick fingers picked at the wood. "Who didn't I kill?

"I'm sure you remember my stories about my sad childhood. Every time I broke a bone, every time I busted someone's face, I was rewarded. They wanted me to love my rage. We have a word for it that best translates to bloodlust. The act of killing is erotic. It is the reason so many warriors fuck each other, because the lust that follows murder is too hot to quench. I never had a lover to share in my lust and hated the feel of it. I answered lust with rage, and so the two built on each other. I did not get this body through magic alone. I became strong as death.

"But I never abandoned my studies. I was obsessed with philosophy and learning new languages. Doronel refugees brought the works of philosophers radically different from anything Ki'an had considered. To them, Ki'an murdered each other not because we were evil or obsessed with death. We killed each other because our culture demanded it. Our governments and religions had created us to be weapons, because it made us easier to control. The second I read that, I understood the wisdom in their words. I grew to hate everything about being a Ki'an.

"My mother added to that hate dutifully as the Geshuri. When I came back from my first military victory at seventeen, she rewarded me by burning all my books. I felt nothing when I bashed her head into the wall, but when my hands wrapped around her neck I felt the rage I feel for my people. My father couldn't talk me out of murdering her and so he fetched my sisters. I didn't hesitate to kill any of them. Each and every one of them were tools of the Geshuri and our glorious Zulan.

"Father had frozen up. He looked at his daughter covered in blood and couldn't even disown her. He hadn't the strength to face combat because he'd been raised to be a coward. I was disgusted by him and everything he represented. So I killed him too. After it was done, I told myself that I'd done it to spare him the pain of living without his children, but I killed him because he was part of the same disgusting system.

"I killed thirty more people that night. They were my neighbors, people who should've been my friends. But they only ever saw me as a mistake of the Gods. Women could be strong and they could know something of war, but their minds were not meant to consider art, machines, or philosophy. They hated me because I was superior to them in every way. Not a single one of them posed the slightest challenge. I saw all their attacks coming and tore them apart.

"None begged for mercy or apologized for how they treated me and I'm glad they didn't.

"After I tore my grandmother's heart out of her chest, I knew my killing spree had to end. Strong as I was, I couldn't fight the might of the Zulan and her army. So I traveled west and tried to get as far away from them as possible.

"I tried to work as a mechanic, but I was too large to pass for a man. The only work I could find was as a guard. When I was done with the job, I was so disgusted with myself that I killed the merchant, his wife and son, and the other three guards he'd hired. I became a robber after that. I took what I wanted. If any women came to stop me, I ended them. If any men couldn't look me in the eye, I thrashed them, and broke a few necks in the process. I was as far from human as you could possibly imagine."

He'd torn off a huge chunk of the wallpaper.

"Still think I shouldn't be killed?" he asked. There was a sadistic glee in his eyes.

The door opened. Torno asked, "Can I-"

"No," Ena snapped. She pushed the door shut with a wave of force.

Vamere cackled. "What? You don't want me to share a whiskey with him anymore?"

"Why are you telling me this?" Ena asked. "You have to know how upsetting this is to hear."

"I'm telling you because you asked. I'm telling the little

girl that used a lake like a toy. Though I'm pretty sure I could snap your neck before you could do anything about it, there's still the chance that you could kill me and truly end the Grand Dream."

"We still have to kill Muttur. I need your help to kill him."

"My evil should persist as a tool to help you achieve good," he cackled. "What a great reason to live."

Ena pinched the bridge of her nose. "How did you change, Vamere? You obviously didn't spend the rest of your life robbing people."

"True. Some gangs and roaming bandits worked hard to recruit me. I tried to live their life but they kept disappointing me. They were little people with little goals. And as horrible as I was, I had no stomach for rape. The sight of it disgusted me. It lead to me to kill my allies. For a time, I devoted my life to finding the ilk of humanity and using my evil for good. That started to fill me with hope. I thought I could have purpose as this ugly finger on the right hand of Justice.

"That's when I met Tishi. She was a Sage. The Gods gave her nightly dreams of me until she traveled hundreds of miles to help me. Before the Gods intervened in her life, Tishi had been a mother of three. Visk killed both of her daughters and sold her and her son back to her husband. Of course by that time, the injuries Tishi's son had suffered were infected and took his life. In mourning, her husband drank himself to death. On the night of her husband's death, Tishi prayed for divine mercy, and the cruel Gods had her dream of me.

"She didn't care if she lived or died. She came to me not as a mother or a warrior, but as a person without purpose. So I felt no hate for her and we were able to be friends. Our journey took us from one side of Ki'an to the other. In that time, I came to feel for her. I dreamt of kissing her and spent every waking moment thinking of a way to take away her pain.

"Another sage found us. Thanil was a healer and surgeon from Duan Si. He'd been given the divine knowledge to lead me through my transformation. So we did. As a woman I'd been death on two legs, but as a man I was given a new purpose. I would unite the world and undo centuries of progress. I was willing to do it, because I hated everything about myself. I didn't care if millions would die to bring me to power. So I drank my first jug of wine and let them transform me.

"I awoke in the middle of the night and found Tishi and Thanil fucking each other's brains out. I don't remember killing them, but I remember the sorrow I felt when I found Tishi dead."

He was working his fingers into the wall beneath the paper. He pulled off chucks of stone and chipped off splinters larger than Ena's fingers.

This was nothing like what Ena expected from his past. He had devoted his life to knowledge, but his past had been so visceral. How had this creature of rage transformed himself into something so virtuous? "How old were you then?" Ena asked.

"Twenty." He smiled at Ena, and she was starting to understand why it was so unsettling. This was the smile of a killer.

"What happened next? You could've called all of Ki'an to you, but you obviously didn't."

"Killing Tishi changed me. It showed me what I had become and what I was going to be. I found all the Sages in Ki'an and killed them. I used their money to buy every book I could and when that money ran out, I went back to killing bandits. There was never a shortage of bandits in Ki'an. Women were bred to kill, and not all of them wanted to give up the spear of steel for the spear of flesh. Killing them made me feel like I was doing some good with my life, but it was another lie.

"I realized then that the greatest lie of all was the Grand Dream. So I went to Mu."

Mu. That's what Ena had forgotten. The city Visk came from, the center of their Geshuri, where the people rose up against their Zulan, that city had been destroyed. "You killed the Geshuri!"

"Every single one I could get my hands on. The rest I had to burn with magic. I burned over a thousand years of religious history. I destroyed monuments to Hultur and every story that spoke of his murders as just. I needed to destabilize the region so Ki'an couldn't involve itself in what was to come. It also gave me all the gold and jewels I would need for my journey because the Geshuri were corrupt as theives.

"I am indeed capable of destroying all of Schlabaum, Ena, but I don't need the energy of the Red Mawnah to do it."

"You heard us," Ena whispered.

His cackling was sinister. "Of course I did. I listen to everything you say. Still think that I'm this friend that you need to save?"

Ena backed into the door and opened it.

Torno put his hand on her shoulder, but she barely felt it. "Ena?"

She shook her head. None of this felt real, but she couldn't wake up. "He destroyed Mu."

"The city?" Visk asked.

Ena nodded.

"It's all gone," he laughed. "I'm curious, Visk. Do you still want to kill me, or have I earned your gratitude?"

Visk pulled out a dagger. She imbued it with red lightning and slashed at the air. Power poured out of her, striking the walls, ripping apart the threshold, and tearing up the hotel's carpet. But the power stopped at his hand. He caught the lightning bolt and all of the flames like they were webs from a spider. With his other hand, he pulled Visk to him and wrapped his hands around her throat. Standing, his head scraped the ceiling, but it broke from where he shoved Visk's body into it.

Debris fell over them as he taunted her. "The great and powerful Visk, made like a doll before the true power of the world! Tell me, warrior, do you feel fear now at last?"

"You don't have to do this!" Ena shouted.

"Do what?"

He tossed the gathered power at the wall behind him. It tore through the floor above them and he pushed out the ceiling. There might've been a bed and furniture as well. He'd taken out the whole wall between them so they had a better view of Visk struggling to breathe. She was trying to move, but he was holding back her limbs with bonds of pure force.

He looked to Visk like he'd forgotten about her. "Oh, *this*. You're right, I don't need to do this, but I figure if I'm going to die I might as well avenge Tishi's family while I'm at it."

"You're not Hultur. Sylene said as much. Spiritually, you're closer to Ngoltur. You are the Wise Ruler. Don't die as a tool to the Gods!"

"Ena, you need to end him," Torno said.

"Listen to him, Ena. Kill me. Or do you not care about Visk?" He pulled Visk up to his ear. "What's that? I can't hear you over the sound of me choking the life out of you."

"You said that you had the strength to kill yourself!" Ena tried. "Remember? If that's really true, then why are you making me do this? Let her go and go out on your own terms."

His scowl shrank. Discerning eyes studied Ena. She pushed on his emotions, feeling for what he was going through. There was guilt at the heart of him. It was consuming him, sucking the life out of every thought before it could form.

"It's not too late to make amends, Vamere." Ena promised him.

He tossed Visk onto the floor. She rolled over and gasped for air. Myrrel was on her, healing the damage to her throat and neck. Sal was there, too, and whatever that hotel had for security would be coming after that. If the Erchritt hotel even had security.

"Vamere is dead. I am no one and nothing. My death will serve no good, but neither has my life. There is no way to balance the scales of justice against the death of a city." He sounded more like his old self, the one who believed in logic and second chances.

There was sorrow pushing in. If she could get him to cry, he might let go of this madness. "Killing Visk won't bring Tishi back, and your death won't make up for taking her life. She's dead. Your parents are dead. Nothing will ever bring them back.

You need to grieve for their loss and move on."

"*They* can't move on," he growled, but the sorrow was coming in.

Ena was only sensing what he was feeling, but if she pushed on his emotions, she risked him figuring out how she was using magic to sway him. This man had been her friend. She needed to believe that he could do this on his own. "I know they can't move on. But if you die, neither can you. You will be a tool of the Gods' will in death. Please. I know you have good in you. You went to find me and talk to me. You believed that peace could be brought about through talking. Believe in the healing power of forgiveness one more time and forgive yourself."

"I never believed in that," he said with chilling calm. He walked back to the hole in the hotel. "Read my journals and you'll see the truth."

And he jumped off the eighth story.

THE FIFTY-FIRST CHAPTER

In Which a New Team is Formed

Magic protected the man that was once Hultur. His sphere of protection pushed back Ena's pillow of air and he fell right through it. By the time she came to the edge there was no sign of him. None on the ground level had seen him either. Hundreds witnessed a massive Ki'an man jump and disappear. Torno suggested that he might've been so powerful that he dematerialized himself, but Ena didn't buy it. He wanted Ena to read his journals to pass judgment on him and she wanted no part in that.

His journals were written in half a dozen languages, and none of them Dorospek. After a lot of talk, Zukoch volunteered to stay behind and work with the Dreamers to decipher the journals of the man who called himself Hultur. He'd been planning to stay behind anyway to "help Kludel and the others settle in." They all knew how Zukoch would be helping. Ena was happy to leave him in Schlabaum.

"Since um...we're all here." Zukoch cleared his throat. They were all gathered by the expansive hotel stable. Only a few stablehands were around but Ena had silenced their circle. "I'd like all of your advice about something."

He sounded serious. Given everything that had happened, Ena was expecting the worst.

"Do you think it's wrong for me to have sex with Kludel?"

"Still?!" Myrrel blurted out. Well, the stablehands knew Ena was silencing them now.

"Kid, you must have the patience of a boulba to not make something happen after all this time." Torno slapped him on the back.

"He is a colt chasing the sunset," Visk said. "Let him do things in his own time. You can do no wrong to her if you exercise patience."

Zukoch nodded. "Sal? Ena?"

"I'm a virgin, man," Sal grumbled. "I don't even know how long boulbas are supposed to wait. Follow your heart and you can't go wrong."

Smiling, Ena brought her hands together. "Listen, Zukoch. You're going to be leaving when we come back and that makes things difficult, right? But she knows this. She's known from the beginning that the two of you were only going to have one night. Then you had four days. Now you might have a week together. If you keep waiting for something to happen, that's all you'll have. You need to have this conversation with Kludel."

Vigorous nodding followed.

"Okay. It's only that...want to do right by her." He was in love. It was clear from the look on his face.

"Speaking of having a week together..." Torno's tone made it clear that he wanted to get back to talks of their mission. "Where are we going?"

"There's nothing we can do about Hultur or Muttur right now. They are faster than us as a group and stronger than us. I still want to try talking to Hultur if we can. Everything he did, he did before he met us, but for right now he needs to be left alone."

No one objected, so she continued. "That leaves us to our new mission: find Muttur's real name. As far as I can tell, he only had two relics when he found us: the Boulba Bracers and the Winged Boots. Since we know where the Boulba Bracers come from, I think our best bet is to go to the treasury that held the Winged Boots." Ena showed the path from Schlabaum to the treasury. It passed right through Tostadt, the city of the dead. Ena left her finger there.

"You wish to destroy this evil." Visk nodded with

approval.

"That place needs to be cleansed. No matter how big of a balebog we're talking about, all of the skeletons will topple if we can destroy the center. I have some plans on how we'll take it out, but this is as good a time as any for everyone to take a break. I'll be coming back to Schlabaum in about a week, hopefully not much longer."

No one else took advantage of this opportunity. They were all willing to die for this cause and Sylene said someone would die.

"In that case, I'll stay here and you can have fun killing a city of skeletons," Ena joked.

They chuckled and didn't hear a woman entering the sphere of silence.

"I want to come." It was Bogelb, the twenty-one-year-old hunter. "I know that I'm not that strong and I can't do magic, but I can speak the language of the land. If Zukoch is staying behind you'll need a translator."

Ena hadn't even thought about that, but the answer was still obvious. "No."

"Why not?" Visk asked. "She has a good head on her shoulders and the heart of a warrior."

"That and she's completely right," added Sal. "It'll be hard enough to get inns without someone who can talk in Dorospek."

"I can handle it," Ena said with confidence. As an example, in Dorospek she said, *"I'd like four rooms and a space for five horses and our wagon."*

Bogelb spoke fast and Ena understood every one in three words.

"I still don't want you to come," Ena insisted.

"I know that you are Ngoltur reborn and that the man who left was Hultur. I am not afraid to die but if I do not travel with you I am not living. Please, let me come." She bowed her head.

They were all staring at Ena. None wanted to tell her no.

"Fine, but you stay out of the fighting unless I say so."

Visk welcomed her with a pat on the back.

"What Bogelb said reminded me of something. I'm not Ngoltur. Sylene, the Grand Dreamer, said that we're all something new. That's part of why I have to find where Muttur came from, to learn who he was before we arrived. We need to know how he thinks if we're going to beat him. Anyway, from now on, we're Team Freedom and I'm Team Leader Ena."

"That sounds horrible." Torno shuddered.

"It sounds like what chewing rocks feels like." Myrrel stuck out her tongue.

"Why are you hunting Muttur?" Bogelb asked. And a very long explanation followed.

~ ~ ~

Team Freedom had a long way to go and so they traveled light. The wagon was left behind and Gale ran so fast that the other horses had to be assisted to match his speed. He had sensed something was off when they returned without the man who wasn't Hultur. Ena did her best to explain with feelings what had happened and eventually the horse stopped looking for him. Gale was best galloping with nothing holding him back. The hardest part was using geomancy to keep the others at his pace. He was a gorgeous animal and Ena loved being back in the saddle with him.

After the first day of traveling with Patches, Torno finally got rid of that horrible creature. Myrrel acted like Narla had some kind of fondness for the animal; she hadn't. Visk seemed to think that selling the three-gait mistake was a bad omen; there was plenty going wrong without that horse. Sal was under the impression that Narla had chosen the beast herself; it was given to them and Narla just jumped on the horse that was closest. Still, Ena found herself giving the horse a long hug goodbye with the rest of them. She hoped he would stop ruining people's lives but suspected he wouldn't.

The new schistrau was supposed to be good for traveling long distances, but Ena was skeptical about what the white-spotted brown bird could do. Zenlauf, the Schistrau, took off like an arrow. Gale rose to the challenge, pushing himself hard to match the speed of the abomination, but for short distances there was no contest. Gale hated it, but Ena couldn't manage pushing two groups of riders ahead at two different speeds. The others could match Gale's speed but he couldn't match Zenlauf.

Still, they'd pass Torno and Gale would slow down and almost prance as he cantered down the road. Zenlauf would pass Gale again and the struggle would begin all over. Torno had to burn a lot of magic, having the Schistrau keep up with Gale's pace and of course he was looking to Ena to restore the Gulda that night at an inn. Back when they were Brokers he might've asked to be restored with a kiss, but he handed her an empty ether crystal.

Bogelb took extralong talking to the locals that morning and wandered back to tell Team Freedom the bad news.

"They say there's only one more town before the road ends. It's a lake town, so they'll have a lot of supplies we need. From the way he was talking, the lost city of Hochel is a death trap." Hochel was the city the balebog Reptear had taken apart.

"Reptear on the road?" asked Ena.

"Bandits. He says a few gangs of marauders are fighting for the rights to Hochel."

"This'll be like driving foxes out with a pack of wolves," Torno grumbled.

"Found another way to look on the worse side of things?" Sal joked.

"Yeah and it ain't funny. If we destroy Tostadt, these marauders will have first claim to Hochel."

"Selfish murderous thieves? They'll be indistinguishable from politicians," Myrrel joked.

Torno took on the affected airs of a politician. "As a bandit, I learned to work with people and have no moral compunctions with manipulating individuals. As you can see, I'm more than qualified to rule."

Ena found enough mirth to smirk. "The plan doesn't

change. Human troubles should be something that Erchritt can handle."

Bogelb raised a hand.

"You can talk," Ena assured her.

"Sorry, I didn't know if I needed permissions or something."

"There's only six of us. Just say your piece as it comes to you."

"It's all part of the Team Freedom way," Myrrel teased.

Torno chuckled.

Ena couldn't believe that they hated her awesome new team name.

"I know how this might sound," Bogelb said, nervously. "But my dad was a bandit when he was younger. He says that most bandits are nothing more than people trying to survive. If they're stealing coin, that means some of them travel into town to buy supplies. If they're stealing people, then they're probably past the point of helping."

"That's good insight. Thank you. Let's ask around on our way to the ruins of Hochel. If these criminals are grabbing coin, we'll minimalize casualties. My hope is that the people of Hochel will want to work with us to destroy the skeletons."

Bogelb looked pleased by Ena's insight.

It was strange to find anyone who thought twice about bandits. Maybe Bogelb would be more useful than Ena thought. Having the opinion of someone who understood bandits might help them find a way to connect to the man who wasn't Hultur. His past as a murdering bandit was haunting, but he'd been their friend for months without showing any sign of malicious intent.

Most Erchrites weren't interested in discussing matters of safety. Though Reptear sightings were handled with severity and focus, discussion about robbers were a little more guarded. Empathic walls shot up and responses grew clipped. Ena lost enthusiasm by the time she'd secured supplies.

A fountain in the town square drew her eyes, the familiar

sight of Muttur' heroism immortalized with him bearing his famed heat shield before a dame in flowing gowns. At closer inspection, the woman had rounded ears and was clearly meant to depict Ngoltur gripped with such overwhelming fear that blood had rushed to her nipples.

Rolling her eyes, she looked around for sympathetic company and found Sal chewing rocks beyond the cobblestone paths. He looked dejected, his brows and arms hanging low on his face. Nearby Leben crafters were constructing an addition to a two story building. The hexagonal roofs overlapping like cells in a hive.

Sal scooted aside along a ditch to give Ena room to sit. "I tried asking if they needed any help, but they couldn't understand me."

"Maybe they want your help but guild laws prevent that," Ena offered more dreamy than sincere.

His scoff came like gravel sliding down a hill. "Pretty sure Erchritt doesn't have builder guilds."

"Oh, they do," Ena was sure. "They wouldn't let me into a hunter's lodge because I'm a woman."

"Glad to know I'm not the only one missing home."

"We all are." Ena rubs his sunbaked arm, there was a good coat of fresh dirt from rolling for hours. "Is something bothering you?"

"Vamere. Or Hultur, or whoever he is now. I was talking to him for hours but I couldn't get through to him. I keep thinking about how nothing I said surprised him or made him reconsider his anger. I know that I don't know empathy magic or anything, but I used to be able to help people. As a Broker I was useful. I saved lives."

"We all did, Sal. And we're going to do that now, only we won't be able to see the lives of those we save. We have to think about the big picture now and the big picture is that our friend didn't destroy the city of Schlabaum and he didn't kill himself. That's because you and Myrrel were there for him."

"You have no way of knowing that."

"I know that you were sincere when you were talking to him."

Sal shrugged which also scrunched up his face. "Ah! You weren't even there."

"I know you, Sal. You're always sincere." She gave him a hug and he lifted his arm up to bring her against his dirt packed cheek.

"Sorry for getting you dirty."

"Stop apologizing for being my friend."

Taking Ena at her word, a great sigh shifted the rocks around his face. That lava core inside got hot enough to heat the soil between the cracks of his face. She stayed there and settled into his earthly warmth, remembering all the days she'd fallen asleep against him in the Broker's wagon.

Team Freedom was able to gather some valuable recon. While he criminals of the region were stealing coin, no one knew much about the state of Hochel. Popular sentiment was the skeletons and reptear had taken over, but humans had been seen coming in and out of the toppled towerscape. Most came by to fence valuables for food, but there were occasions when battered bodies stumbled out of the ruins, their faces haunted by the life inside.

As the road evolved from packed dirt to boulba smoothed stone, the edge of civilization was marked by a makeshift sign on the road. Originally it had read, *All Dead. Turn Back.* Someone had tagged it to read, *City of Dead. Join the Black.* Others had added pictures of penises and boobs.

Before them, the main road into Hochel was blocked with a large gate of wooden spears and rocks. It was simple matter for Ena to push the rocks aside, but before she could burn open the gate, a deep voice called out.

"One more spell and you'll find an arrow!" the voice threatened in Faulchet. It was definitely a man's voice. The baritone timber had quite the presence to it.

Torno readied his deathstaff, Visk her spear, and Myrrel had her wand at the ready.

"Reveal yourselves," Ena cried out.

"Nope. Turn around and leave."

Ena had a general idea where he was in the tall buildings at the edge of the city. She tried reaching out with empathy, felt nothing, and imagined her senses rolling over the space like a sheet caught in the wind. Fear rumbled against the sheet, and she felt the shiver of at least seven.

"Right building," Ena told Torno.

He was already aiming. "I see 'em."

"Come talk. We're not leaving," Ena shouted to the bandit in his native Faulchet.

"He says they have eyes all over the woods and they're threatening to end us," Bogelb translated.

"I come to remove the blight of the balebog. We need the help of those that live in Hochel." Ena hoped she'd said that right. Bogelb gave an affirming nod.

"Then you have come to die," the deep voice taunted. Ena caught enough of it to get the gist.

With her left hand a single gesture faster than her right, she tore off the front of the four floors she was sure the bandits had holed up in. The spell to follow sucked the hidden scouts out of the building. Though it hadn't flushed out all the bandits, it tossed five of them into the air. Torno caught a volley of arrows from the woods with a wall of air, and Ena caught the falling bandits with a net of force. Short bodies swam in the panic of being unfamiliar with levitation.

A tall, lanky one was suspended upside down. The Leben man couldn't be older than seventeen. His eyes were marked black with soot, dirt, ash, or some combination of the three. They had all painted some part of their faces black and none looked older than twenty.

"Call them off or my friend will start burning the trees," Ena threatened.

Visk imbued her spear with red lightning and directed her attention towards the archers in the trees, still uselessly firing into Torno's wall.

After Bogelb translated, a short girl with half her face painted black told him, "Let them in." Her skin was puffy with the eye on the painted side of her face was fused shut by untreated burn marks.

The lanky man called out in his deep bellow, "Stand down! Open the gate."

Ena dropped the kids in soot painted faces. "I take it you're the Black?"

The short leben girl with a burnt face nodded. "I'm Fox, that's Hooper." She pointed at the lanky speaker with a deep voice. Half a dozen others were named. They all had simple names like soldier monikers.

Snake, an archer from the woods who couldn't be younger than twenty-five, had the look of a teacher. The older Leben was chiding teenagers as they picked up their arrows from where they'd hit the wall of air. One of them grumbled about having never fought magic before and Snake smacked the kid in the side of the head. The sight of it made Ena's blood boil, but they were here to find allies.

"Come," said Fox. "Night will want to see you."

As much as the city had been torn apart, most of the towers still stood solid. Debris had been collected to block passage down streets but the main trails were swept nearly clean. The group had to follow through the ruins of buildings where more guards in black waited. Getting a better look at them, Ena not only saw signs of sowing and embroidery, but freshly dyed ramie fabric. This group of teenagers was organized.

Fox sent the sentinels hand signals as they went, but her mood remained steady.

Empathy magic was flying around as they traveled; most of it spread out like a pulse between the members of the Black. At every checkpoint they sensed each other's intent and responded without a single gesture. Beyond fear, there was a noticeable feeling of awe directed towards Ena. These children had seen her peel a tower like a potato. They believed in her.

Fox hung back to issue Ena a clear warning, "Night is our king. Show him respect or I'll poison your blood."

Night had set up his command center in what might've been an outdoor marketplace or town square. There was plenty of room to stand around, lots of tables to sit and enjoy the stew, and a large, gaudy throne that sat a modest thirty feet off the ground. The makeshift dais had clearly once been a two-story building, and had a star painted backdrop resting on the back to give it the illusion of being a throne itself.

The man who went by Night was wide for a Leben, built more like a Fieta than an Erchritt. Both of his cheeks were painted, giving the illusion that his face sat on a thinner, vertical rectangle of blue. On his person was a sparkling coat of interwoven knick knacks that may have once been jewelry bands. On his head sat a grand crown of black iron, accented with spikes of working light crystals. With such an audacious crown and an absurd throne, the man had to be joking.

Night sent out a push of lust at Ena and winked at her. Ena replied with a shove of what she hoped was unimpressed disgust. That brought a smile to his face and there was a charm to that grin. He wasn't alone on the raised platform. On one side, a bare-chested Leben woman waited with a vase of wine. On the other side, a Ki'an woman waited on a smaller throne with a bare-chested man serving her. The Ki'an wore a crown of her own with three light crystals and a very tall mug shaped into a leaping salmon.

"Dismount," shouted Hooper.

They looked to Ena and she complied.

Hooper led them to bow and only when every head dipped did Night stand.

"All hail the King of Night," Hooper called out, and the gathered procession echoed, "Hail!"

"Who brings me these trinkets?" Night asked. The pompous pissant sounded like a teenager playing a game. Hooper's oration commanded more attention by a wide margin. Night's voice was far too nasally to be taken seriously, but then, there he was on a throne of repurposed metal and colorful blankets.

"I do," announced Fox.

"Black Fox, rise and face the Eyes of Night."

She did as she was bid. "They tampered with the gate and announced their intention to enter Tostadt. We gave warning, but when they would not leave, they overwhelmed us with magic." She pointed to Ena. "Her especially."

"You may all rise." A wicked grin played on his goofy face. "Black Touched! Many have mocked my prophecies in secret. You may deny it but the Ears of Night hear all. That laughter will cease on this night and all nights that follow. There stands before you Dawn, the prophesied savior of the land. So comes the Dawn!"

"So comes the Dawn!" they echoed.

The Ki'an woman rose. She said something to Night and he shook his head. His words eased her fears and then brought a whole slew of new ones.

"Ena, is this another title of Ngoltur?" Sal asked in too much more than a whisper.

She shook her head. "This is all new to me."

The self-styled King of Night clapped his hands to get everyone's attention. "Black Touched! We shall welcome Dawn with a great feast, and then we will march. At long last we will see the end of night. Long is the Night!"

"Long is the Night!" they echoed.

"But longer will be the day. All will be tested. All will know blood either as it spills from your guts or as it quenches your blades! Dawn has come and the great war can at last begin! So comes the Dawn!"

"So comes the Dawn!" they echoed.

"And so too comes glory. All may eat their fill. All on street duty and clean up and latrine jobs will work no more today and tomorrow! All imprisoned are released! The Black Touched are united on this day and we will all bask in the glow of The Dawn!"

They cheered and hollered. People were jumping up and

down to celebrate. "So comes the Dawn," they chanted. And the chants continued as a great revelry overtook them.

"Ena, this is weird, right?" Bogelb asked once she was sure she wouldn't have to translate any more.

"Yeah, this is weird."

THE FIFTY-SECOND CHAPTER

In Which Team Freedom
Meets the Black

Barrels of wine were rolled out and served to any who could produce a cup. Fresh deer were brought in and roasted, and the crowd challenged each other to make songs about waiting for the venison. The Black Touched all took turns cooking, playing instruments, and cleaning out dishes for more to use. Night might have been a bombastic blowhard, but he'd organized the ruins of Hochel into something like a town.

The King of Night wouldn't parley with Ena deeming instead to lounge atop his throne of pomp and decay. Occasionally, the half-naked woman beside him would sit upon his lap and he'd kiss and fondle her or lick wine off her taut belly. It was an abhorrent sight that Ena's lurid curiosity couldn't abandon. She kept checking to see if they intended to fuck before his gathered procession. Thankfully, the man disappeared before *that* happened.

Night might've been the only one to engage in anything like romance. The gangly Hooper had eyes Bogelb who seemed to enjoy the company of the older Snake. It was very likely that three more people had their eyes directed on those three and all that confusion was bound to make a great many people frustrated by the night's end.

Visk had found the company of their Queen of the Moon, who they simply called Moon. The man that accompanied Moon was indeed her manservant. She kissed him to kill time, grabbing at his crotch to accent her jokes. None of this turned Visk off to her company, but neither was she interested in kissing Moon. Ki'an culture was indeed a complicated mystery.

With festivities high, it wasn't long before a Gulam man in his early twenties grabbed Ena's attention. The sight of his dark skin and round ears was a welcome sight, but the man was an immigrant from Duan Si. Bad as Ena's Faulchet was, her Duanspek might've actually been worse. So she found herself playing guitar for the crowd, mangling the atrocious Schistrau's Song and other Erchritt favorites. Undeterred, the handsome man encouraged her to dance. Flung from one dance partner to the next, all assaulted her with empathic licks of interest but she hadn't the finesse to turn them down without hurting their pride. Teenage boys and twenty-something men turned their affections elsewhere, but one of the dancers hadn't given up.

Torno cut through the crowd and held out a hand to her. "Can I have this dance?"

Ena stepped into his arms. "Have you come to save me?"

Warmth cracked his lips. "Of course. Without my help you might actually have a good time."

Giggled, she leaned onto his chest. "I am having a good time. Though I'm not sure how much more of this attention I can take."

"You're still not used to center stage?" The flirt managed to sound surprised.

"I miss running back to our wagon and hiding until morning."

"I'm glad you aren't hiding." He let out a content sigh. "Your smile is infectious, you know that?"

Ena pulled back to make an appalling face that showed teeth. "This smile?"

"That's the one." He tried to put on the same face, but he quit fast and smiled warm as he ever looked at Kalta.

"Can I ask you about your exes?" Ena said softly.

He regarded her with an easiness. "Believe it or not, I don't want to keep secrets from you. If there's something you wanna know about me, ask."

"Did you love Kalta?"

"I still do."

"Even now?"

Laughter born of self-depreciation escaped his lips. "Pretty sad, huh? There's this optimistic part inside of me thinks that she's given up hunting us. A more pathetic part of me imagines her showing up and apologizing. She doesn't just apologize to you, but she apologizes for everything she's done to me. I dreamt that she helped us fight Muttur and we returned to the Capital to right all the wrongs we'd ever done."

"I can take you off the team," Ena offered.

"You're not getting rid of me that easily."

"I meant when we fight Kalta."

Torno gave a long sigh. He glanced out at the happy Blacks. "I'm ready to kill her. That's why I keep dreaming about her. You still haven't learned how to drift. We haven't had a lesson in...well, a while. I'm the only one who stands a chance of stopping Kalta in a duel and I know it's not much of one."

"It won't be a duel," Ena promised. "We'll all be there. Together we can take her."

That eased his fears, but only enough for him to put his fake swagger smile on. "You wanted to ask me about Fascinosa too."

Ena blushed.

"Did you like watching us kiss?" He whispered into her ear.

She slapped his chest and then leaned into him. She could feel his heart beating on her cheek. "You hurt him, didn't you?"

"Deeply." He got quiet.

"Did you and him talk about me?"

"He asked me if it was okay if he married you."

"What did you tell him?"

The slow song came to an end and the Black Touched applauded. People were switching instruments and getting lost in a discussion of what to play. Torno kept his eyes on the activity.

"Torno, I want to know," she gave him a light shove.

"I told him that I wouldn't get in the way of you and him, but that I wasn't over him. I'll admit it, before we boarded the boat, I thought that was going to be my chance to win him back." He sounded pained.

"Torno, I'm sorry."

"It wasn't your fault. I got hurt by Kalta and he got to know you. It's only natural that he'd fall in love with you. Everyone does. I think it's easier to know that. It makes me feel like less of a fool for throwing myself at you for almost two years." He was close enough for Ena to see his dark cheeks flushing. Maybe she could only see Torno blushing because she knew his face so well.

"It was three years," Ena insisted.

"It was two," he argued.

The music started up again. It was a smooth melody with a woman singing soft as a cloud in the night's sky. The music took them, swaying the pair back and forth again. He moved her without saying a word and Ena trusted him to lead them far from people reclining on the floor. He was fixated on her, his eyes never straying.

"Two and a half," he conceded. "I didn't start liking you until you started going to parties. I only wanted to be your friend before that."

"This coming from the man who said you loved me at first sight?"

Torno chuckled. "Okay, love might've been a little too strong of a word. You stilled my heart. I'd never seen someone as beautiful as you."

"Liar," she giggled.

Nerves were hard to swallow down. She should tell him about the Romance Escape. She should tell him about how she'd heard about him and seen him before they ever even met. He deserved to know.

The music kicked up the tempo. Torno picked her up and spun her around. He kept smiling to encourage some levity. He guided her out to work her feet and brought her back close with expert finesse. She'd learned how to dance with him and now that they were dancing again, Ena couldn't find the words to tell him to stop. One more dance and then she would tell him the truth of why she hated him.

That one dance lasted half the night.

"Ena, I got some bad news." He glanced over at the band. They were all calling it quits. Nearly everyone had moved to some other part of the ruins of Hochel. "This dance must come to an end."

"Oh," she pulled back and scratched at where her long black wig met her scalp. "That's probably for the best. My feet are tired," she lied. Healing her feet was a matter as trivial as restoring solar fatigue.

"I'm gonna see if they have any of that venison left." He left her side and took in his surroundings. So fast his attention faded from her. There was this bashful quality in his face made hard as he walked away.

"I heard about you and Kalta," she blurted out. Ena realized that didn't really make any sense. "Through the great goss. I saw you and her together in dreamcasts and I...I was rooting for you two. I thought you would have children and grow old together and when I heard that you cheated on her, it...um...You remember when we first met in person? I was mad at you for breaking Kalta's heart. I was mad at you for a long time because I thought you were the person that Kalta said you were."

"Listen," he sounded pained. He couldn't even look at her. "I know. I figured it out when you kept calling her Kalta. You don't have to apologize for hating me back then. I deserved your hate. I still do and I'm honestly touched that you've forgiven me."

Ena ran up to meet his eyes.

He was so sad. Those dark eyes of his looked blacker than the night sky. There was no life in them. "One day I'll live up to your forgiveness. I promise."

Ena couldn't follow him. She was struck by the depth of

his pain. She felt it without using a kiss of empathy and it swallowed her. He didn't know how important he was to her. He didn't know that she cared so much about him that she was willing to look past the bullying and the sleeping around and even his fake swagger that he thought made him charming. He didn't know that Ena was in love with him.

Sylene whispered his name and reflected Ena's own feelings back at her. Hearing his name should've filled her with disgust and resentment, but it was all sweetness and forlorn. She wanted him to hold her hand and tell her that everything was gonna work out. She wanted him to find her in the middle of the night and listen to all of her thoughts about life. She wanted to hear how his thoughts had changed. She wanted to wake up next to him and start every day with that wonderful smile.

That was the moment to follow him and confess her feelings, but she was frozen; so was their love.

~ ~ ~

Sleep refused to come and ease Ena's heart. She replayed every sweet moment with him. She dwelled on the first time he took her hand or that time he gallantly lowered her to the floor and laughed even when she slapped him. She wanted to remember the first time he tried to kiss her, but it was lost in a sea of dozens of similar moments. For some reason, she recalled him coming within a few inches before she stuck out her tongue and called him disgusting. Those words were burrowing into her heart now and he had every right to throw them back in her face.

"Dawn," came the deep voice of Hooper. It was so deep, Ena hardly recognized it as a voice at first.

She threw on a jacket to hide the fact that she wasn't wearing a bra. The blue skin cream. She couldn't open the door without putting that on. "Yes."

"Night awaits you. I've come to escort you."

"I will need half an hour."

"I'll be waiting."

Fat lot of good that did her. She cast haste and got herself as clean as she could without having a proper bath. "Take me to him."

"No problem." He cleared his throat, but his pitch hardly changed. "Sorry about that; morning voice."

Hooper led her to a gutted tower. It was hard to tell if the place had been an apartment or some kind of business before the disaster the Reptear brought, but there was a large courtyard at the base. The Black Touched had set up a perimeter to guard their King. They paid Ena no mind, even the Gulam man who'd danced with her the night before.

Night was watching the rising sun from the second floor. He looked to be standing before a window, but his black cape fluttered in the breeze. Ena got a good view of the man's hairy blue chest. Scars criss-crossed his front, favoring his left side. Two scars looked to be near fatal wounds to his heart and a third might've gutted him.

"Morning, Dawn." He glanced back to make sure Hooper was gone. "Or do you go by Ngoltur?"

"Ena will do fine. Who told you I was Ngoltur Reborn?"

Night shook his head. "That's not important. I'm sorry about keeping my distance last night. I had an image to maintain and I had been looking forward to my night with Black Ferret."

"Your sex slave?" She didn't bother to hide her disapproval.

"No one here is a slave. We've lost hundreds to desertion and at times it nearly crippled us." He shook away his defensive tone. "Being a sex servant is a great honor. The Black Touched have to wait weeks for their turn."

"Being your fuck toy is a great honor?" Ena arched a brow.

"They have no work to do. They have the right to refuse me or any other that wants their time. And it is a great pleasure to serve others. Maybe that's a pleasure you've never known."

Ena remembered stroking Obi off. She looked away to hide any signs of blush. "It isn't important who told you I was Ngoltur Reborn, but it's worth your time to defend your cult's sexual practices?"

Night glided across the room to meet her gaze. "Of course."

Ena crossed her arms and steadied her breathing. "And why is that?"

"Because all of this is for you." His smile became toothy.

"Me?"

"Ena, I've known you were coming for over five years. I left my job, my family, and my dog behind to make sure there was an army here to help you." His voice was practically cracking. He lacked the diction of a leader or even a soldier.

"You're a Sage! You've been dreaming about my coming to Hochel." She took another look outside at everything he'd done. The place was defensible. There were hundreds, maybe even a thousand people all working together. "Why didn't you go to the Dreamers?"

"I tried, but the Dreamers obviously didn't know anything. When I got around to visiting Schlabaum I couldn't get past the tourist trap. No one would let me talk to the Dreamers, no one would help me. So I realized that I needed to be a Sage that helped you fight. Now, what would you ask of me?"

"Well, I'm curious about the throne and all the weird names."

He nodded. "I grew up in Vergebaum Heff. We have a colosseum there. The fighters took on these larger than life personalities and all of their fans could recognize each other at a glance. Even after my family moved to Karzak, my Dad could always find people from Vergebaum Heff because of the bright shirts he owned from the colosseum.

"I knew that things were going to be bad when the Reptear attacked, but I had no idea how hard it would be to keep spirits up. Between the skeletons and the Reptear, we were going to break. I needed something to keep morale up and I came up with this crazed idea for everyone to wear the black ashes of a city destroyed. We came up with initiation trials to earn a new name, they received their marks and suddenly we weren't a band of survivors, we were The Black!

"I knew if I told them everything about you and the future they'd think I was another fake sage, so I invented a story about the night and the coming dawn and it helped to rally us together. Those that hated it joined up with other groups, but that was fine for me. We needed loyal fighters to lead you through Hochel. All of this is here to bring you safely to Tostadt so that you can fulfill your destiny and destroy the balebog."

Ena remembered what Sylene said about Ena having one of two choices. Ena had made a third choice. Something about his vision didn't make any sense. "What if I never came?"

"Then we would've stayed here until I died," he shrugged. "Or I guess until you died. To be honest, I was starting to worry. About three weeks back I stopped dreaming about your arrival and that hadn't happened before. Did something bad happen? Is that why Narla and Hultur aren't with you?"

She ran her finger over the fake scalemail on her jacket's side. "Narla is dead. I don't know where Hultur is."

"I'm sorry."

She didn't want his sympathy. There was too much that she needed to figure out and this wasn't helping. "So you've gathered this army to serve me?"

"That's right. I'm here to serve you too if you need some company." He kissed the air.

"Did that work in any of your dreams?"

"Not really, but sometimes you kiss me-" Night stopped himself from saying something more.

Ena was fine with him having secrets. "What if I tell you to take all of these people and escape to Schlabaum?"

Night shook his head. "It's too late for that. We've had to kill, steal from towns, and rob merchants to stay where we are. No matter what happens, this is their home. After you destroy the balebog and scare off the Reptear, Hochel will be claimed by the Black. It's our destiny now and we made it by our own hands."

Ena wasn't sure what to make of this man. "How old are you? You sound like a kid."

"I'm twenty-five."

"Sorry," she muttered.

"I used to work the mines before I came to Erchritt. I never learned how to be a leader. I just had to make this work. I do things a little different, but I like it." He was staring wistfully into the streets. "I know my soldiers are young but the Black are ready for this war, I know they are. We will escort you safely to Tostadt."

"Wait, you're not going to be helping me in the City of the Dead?"

Night shook his head. "In my dreams, you told me that it wasn't my place to fight the Reptear. Our purpose is to clear a path to the edge of the balebog. That'll mean a fight with our old enemies-the Crooked Rakes."

"Do they all carry rakes or something?"

Night was oblivious. "Huh? No, that would be silly."

"Night!" Hooper called out from down below. Fox had met up with him. "We got prisoners. Looks like they came all the way from Gulambar."

"Friends of yours?" Night asked.

Ena shrugged and followed.

~ ~ ~

The path to the prisons was filthy. Caltrops of debris added to the grime and made escaping not only slow, but potentially deadly. Piles of trash had dubious stability and if someone lost their footing and tripped, they could easily fall face first into a spike. Hanging cages lay empty, their inhabitants freed to honor the coming of Dawn. But there were blood and fecal stains from where the prisoners had suffered. For all his talk of not having slaves, Night sure did like to force people to do as he pleased.

Snake walked in with two prisoners. They were tied to a pole, the back and front carried by teenagers. The pair from Gulambar were in black outfits accented with gold trimmed pauldrons and chest plates. Somehow, against all reason, they'd been followed all the way to Hochel. Their prisoners were none other than Cerrano and Iodize, the Junior Mages.

THE FIFTY-THIRD CHAPTER

In Which the Black Marches

Cerrano and Iodize had seen better days. Their skin wasn't dirty, it was dirt. From the look of the cuts on their uniforms and the damage to their ornamental armor, they'd run into every Reptear from Vergebaum Heff to Hochel. They looked malnourished, Iodize especially so, and Cerrano was suffering from some kind of rash on her neck. For people who were supposed to be a threat, they looked about as pathetic as they possibly could. Ena had the poles they were tied to planted in the ground. She might've had them untied if she thought they could stand. Team Freedom assembled and the gags in the Junior Mage's mouths were removed.

"It looks like you two bit off more than you can chew," Ena said with more mirth than pity.

"I don't need to chew. I can swallow you whole!" Iodize tried to demonstrate. He looked like a duck chomping at the air.

"Your lives are as good as forfeit," the haughty Cerrano promised. "If you lay down and surrender now we, the great and powerful *Senior* Junior Mages, will spare you the humiliation of death."

"Well, we're not Senior Junior Mages yet," Iodize mumbled to his partner.

"Yes, we are! Kalta said if we found Ena Vamqinsys we'd be promoted to Senior Junior Mages. We found her, so we're Senior Junior Mages."

"Don't we need to officially be promoted before it's official."

Ena glanced back at her friends.

"I think we should kill them." Torno turned his attention to the prisoners. "You two are like Cannegurin, you know that? Those are humans that work with Reptear and feed off their scraps."

"That's disgusting!" Iodize replied.

"Now adding reprehensible behavior unbecoming of a Broker to your list of offenses," Cerrano said with a sadistic grin.

"They more a threat to themselves than us," Ena said to her friends.

"Hey!" Cerrano barked. "Don't ignore me. I outrank you, you upjumped farm girl!"

"Did you two box heads miss the part where she threw a lake at an army?" Torno snapped.

"Your lies won't impress us!" Iodize replied. "We will take you back to Kalta and then to the Supreme Magus to receive justice!"

"I've had more than enough of the Supreme Magus's justice, thank you very much," said Myrrel.

"It seems unwise to simply release them," argued Visk. "They continue to find us. If we let them go, they will surely find us again."

"We could take them with us back to Doronel. It's not Caredor, but they could find their way home," suggested Sal.

It unsettled Ena that she only had these four to bounce ideas off of. She was feeling the loss of Narla, Zukoch, and even Hultur. "Bogelb?"

"I don't really understand who these two are," she admitted. "They were peacekeepers who want to punish you for abandoning your posts?"

"That and we incited rebellion, attacked a superior officer, and killed a governmental head," Torno told her.

"The fools have confessed!" Cerrano declared victoriously.

"Adding these crimes to the mental ledger!" Iodize shouted, his voice giving out from the strain.

"They just look sad, beaten, and hungry," Bogelb said.

Ena nodded. "I like Sal's plan of taking them prisoner. We can pick them up on our way back." There were no objections. "Wash them, feed them, and get them some fresh clothes before throwing them in a cell."

The Black didn't move until Night echoed Ena's command.

"You'll regret this," Cerrano fumed. "We will be your end!"

"I won't regret this, I'm hungry."

"Iodize! Do not show any sympathy for the enemy!"

"You smell too. I didn't want to say anything, but I saw you step in that pile of shit."

"Me? You haven't cleaned your teeth in over a week! Scratching your teeth doesn't do anything..."

They continued to bicker as they were carried off.

Ena registered Torno's displeasure and couldn't help but chortle. "It's the right thing to help them."

"It might be the humane thing, but with them here, Kalta won't be far behind. We still don't even know how they keep finding us," Torno grumbled.

"They didn't know about Ena using the lake." Myrrel put on an optimistic smile. "Maybe Kalta's given up the chase."

"Kalta is an Archmage. The last we saw her, she was pursuing with an army of five hundred combatants," Visk told Bogelb.

"That sounds bad."

Night walked over with a flourish of his cape. "Are you ready to ride into battle?!"

Ena shifted away from the man and his zealous eyes. "Why am I suddenly afraid to say, 'yes?'"

~ ~ ~

Being escorted by the Black Touched felt more like being in the middle of a parade than an army. War drums and trumpets blared, announcing the coming of Dawn with great fanfare. Bannerholders waved plain black flags back and forth. Pikers and shieldbearers marched in formation to block for the

King of Night, the Queen of Moon, and all of Team Freedom. The display was so grandiose that when arrows started to fly, Ena thought they might've been streamers. But these were weapons of war and soon blood was streaming on the paved causeway.

The army was spread out enough to scout the Crooked Rakes early and on all sides. Signals came faster than Ena could follow and the young army ran into buildings to fight and die. Arrows flew out from every angle and the Black's evokers stopped volley after volley. Torno and Visk added their support, blasting at well stationed archers in the ruins of Hochel's towers.

Night signaled the procession to stop. Before them, the road widened as it grew near a great statue before a civic center. Panicked bodies flooded the streets in egress, their arms full of whatever supplies they could grab. The frenzy of activity made it hard to tell foe from fleeing non-combatant, but the enemy came in force.

Junk adorned soldiers tested Night's flanks. Bodies slammed into shields. Pikes met legs. Cleavers connected with shoulder blades. Hooks pulled people off the defensive lines and dragged them into apartments turned into abattoirs. Upper windows and balconies gave archers and casters an abundance of room to snipe.

Ena's had been advised to work as a counter caster. Surrounding the airspace with eels of pure electricity, she commanded the school to intercept ethereal strands with a single flowing arm. Her free hand gathered the released effects, powered them up, and sent the spells back towards the caster. Loosed arrows were pushed back with raw force, adding more bricks to the ever crumbling city.

Sniper fire ceased and Ena sent the eels through the buildings. Screams marked the ends of lives, and their forces pushed out with desperation. Shield-bearers wavered, exposing Night's guard, but Sal pushed out. Every punch made a difference, shattering makeshift spears and pikes like branches on a sapling. His push gave the shield-bearers time to rally and they the stepped up to protect his retreat.

Drums signaled marching orders. Rear squadrons rushed in to cut down wounded and break the spirit of the remaining Crooked Rakes that once lay in ambush. The Black broke formation to charge excavated buildings. Teenagers came out with blades covered in gore and comrades propped up on shoulders. The Black came to a stop. Myrrel sucked in a purple gulda and healed. Without any snipers in sights, Ena dismissed the eels, leaving Gale to observe Myrrel work.

Three spells flew out in tandem. One was a raw bolt of electricity. Ena grabbed the splitting bolt and whipped it into the wand cast strands of ether. Fire and darkness bloomed in the sky. Torno shot down the three casters in rapid succession, flashes of light marking the end to a rare caster in Leben Erde.

Troops screamed to bolster courage and the youths pushed to take the statue without any major confrontations. Held by the mostly chestless statue was the Crooked Rake of this faction's namesake. It lay in a bent arm of bronze, the metal having been melted into a near solid shape that barely resembled a human form. Around the statue were signs of command. Pots, blankets, bottles, musical instruments, and military figurines lay among the debris.

Barking took Ena's attention away from the loss. Shouts answered back. Beast and humans became indistinguishable once more. A large swath of the Black's main advance pushed into a single alley. Raised shields made from dressers and doors blocked hails of arrows and knives, but bodies were left behind screaming. Ena reached out to gather arrows into a cyclone of wind before sending them into the windowless floors where the attackers hid. Wind walls weren't being cast anymore. The Black had depleted their ether.

"To me!" Moon shouted and the shaken forces rallied behind the fearless Ki'an.

Shields and pikes were passed back to the rear squadron. There were too many teenagers in that bunch. Some of them looked no older than thirteen. Bandages were wet with blood, many wrapping up their fellows even as they marched. Yet the younger they were, the less they seemed to fear. They were proud to hold a shield and prouder still to be sent into the heart of the fighting.

"Starboard flank!" Torno called out a second before shooting an engulfing blast from his deathstaff. Twenty figures or more were covered in flames.

More pushed in, striking out at the Black's weakened side. Women and teenagers lead this assault, the lot of them ragged and desperate. Rocks flew over shields. Pikes were gripped and pushed back. The Black's defenses were breaking. Teenagers who had danced and flirted met their end to bits of metal tied affixed to poles.

Ena manifested a Slizzer of solid cold. The scythe-armed worm came into full view with an illuminating light of blue. Light and cold cut through adult and child indiscriminately. There simply wasn't any way for Ena to spare the young. Her monster of elemental triggered a primal reaction of fear and their spirits broke. Crooked Rakes ran away screaming.

Dancing with Torno didn't want to leave Ena's mind. The node had worked so well to power her spell of light. The shivering fear within made her look to his face, hoping for some sign of his heart. If he thought of anything more than a tactical consideration, his eyes didn't show it. This wasn't the time to talk, but the ebb in the fighting made it hard for Ena to focus.

"Ena!" Myrrel bellowed with magical volume.

She dismounted to see to the wounded.

"If you can't save 'em move on," Myrrel snapped. She was focused, not a flake of fear in her voice.

Ena looked from the slit neck of a fourteen-year-old boy to a girl of fifteen holding her guts. She was still alive as Ena turned her attention to another. A wound in the shoulder wasn't beyond Ena's power. The bleeding could be stopped. She recited the incantation and imagined the glyphs as she slid ether from reconnecting veins to managing the flow of blood. A wet hand grabbed Ena's elbow. She couldn't spare to look back at the dying girl who held her. Satisfaction flowed into Ena when the worst of the shoulder wound was healed and she was rewarded with the feel of the girl's hand lifelessly letting go.

"Her," Myrrel said with a point. She pointed to a vibrant teenager. Her lips were painted black and her wide eyes were shattering. A chipped blade in her head had cut most of her brow.

"Save him!" a boy cried out.

He grabbed Myrrel by the shoulders, physically pulling her off her patient. Her hand was inside their chest. "Sal!"

Sal was there to push them back. Visk helped to shove others back as the wounded were carried in on bloody stretchers and sagging shoulders. Hundreds watched Ena and Myrrel work and it seemed like every hand in the army was urging them to help their friends. Ena had to close her eyes to force their pleading voices out of her mind. Myrrel thought Ena could save this girl. She needed to focus.

But as she struggled to work through slowing the girl's heart and mental functions, she seized. The blade slipped in deeper and Ena moved on to another body, and another. So few of them were adults and so many of them were boys. It didn't help to know that Leben Erde favored sending men into combat. The gender of the dead only started to matter as Ena's diagnosis spell attuned her with the bleeding.

Death was settling into the minds of the Black. Those children so filled with bloodlust were devolving into panicked muddles of mourning. Only the rare adults in the mix had anything like a look of stoicism and they used that emotional shield to rally the survivors back into formation.

Ena and Myrrel had either saved all the dying or their corpses had been removed. Dozens of injured lay before them. Everyone who could stand were sent back to the fighting. Lives saved, Ena crawled over a bloody bodies to work her hands onto a long gash threatening an arm. Myrrel couldn't follow. Her shoulders were limp, her eyes unfocused.

"What's wrong with her?"

"No more gulda," Sal explained. He was pouring water into

her mouth.

"Ena, we need to keep moving," Torno put in a shift of deference, but he wanted to give the order.

She couldn't look away from the injured. They were so scared and so damn young. Even those who were twenty looked so much younger than her. She'd never felt so old or so helpless. "Why, so we can go back to killing people?!"

"Yes," answered Visk. She held out a blood spattered hand. "Women rise to every challenge."

Ena gripped the red skin with a hand soaked in blood. Visk pulled her to her feet. "Women rise to every challenge," Ena echoed. The familiar mantra actually helped to settle her. They were in a battle. All of this was expected. Without her help, more would die. Of course with her help, much more would die. She mounted Gale and rode to rejoin the Black.

Night and Moon didn't need much from Team Freedom. The morale of the Crooked Rakes was shattered. Once Team Freedom returned to their position in the center, they were marching forward unimpeded. They'd left Crooked Rakes turf and were entering the territory of the people they called "Licks." No people called Licks could be decent even by bandit's standards. Before Ena had a chance to see what this next threat would be, a body hit the floor.

Myrrel had literally fallen off her horse.

She was bruised from the fall, but nothing that needed healing. The real problem was that Myrrel hadn't just exhausted her ether reserves, she'd overdrawn channeling ether from her deepest sources and now she might go into full shock. Ena needed to act quickly and decisively. Feeling the motion of her ribs, she waited for an exhale and laid her lips on Myrrel. A mouth to mouth transfer of ether was theoretically simple, but required a still mind. No nodes. No emotions to risk flavoring the ether to something that could rattle a spirit. Among the death, the shouting, the fear that Myrrel's body would fail, Ena had to settle her heart to numb and breathe.

Fighting broke out around them and Myrrel opened her

eyes. "I'm flattered, but I only go for guys," she croaked.

Ena laughed. "You'd make an exception for me." She helped her back to her feet.

Red lightning streaked overhead popping a strand of indigo. Darkness spread out, threatening to engulf Night, Team Freedom, and way too many teenagers who had no business being in a fight like this. Ena took control of the spreading darkness with her bracelets. Shaped into an alligator of light dimming entropy, the beast chomped buildings, eroding stone, cracking glass, and ending whoever had been inside.

The Licks weren't fighting directly but harrying their forces with quick attacks before retreating. These were adult men with real steel, and they had no trouble overpowering the Black at every engagement. Only numbers favored the Black, but the Licks were relentless.

Visk and Sal ran out to fight in the thick of it. Torno switched out his deathstaff and the fool rushed into the fray with his sword. He wasn't Visk. He didn't have a lifetime of fighting in a melee, but then again, neither did these teens. There was no time to protect him. Too much was happening for Ena to protect everyone.

Ena needed to attack.

There was plenty of fear to draw on. All Ena had to do was reach out and tap a person to feel that fear. Empathy triggered sympathetic feelings in her and she drew on that to power a great crab of cold. It worked quicker than thinking about a node and kept her fear undiluted. The foreign-born emotions were enough to make Ena panic. She used that panic to fuel force and she erected a wall on their north side, blocking off much of the Lick's territory.

Pinching at every soldier in good armor, the cold crab flung Licks about like ants and balled them up in preparation to eat. Night pointed out a building with few Blacks around the ground floor. One enlarged swing of the crab's pinch struck the base, ripping off a support pillar. Bricks seemed to shout when they fell. But then stone didn't scream and even if it did, Ena was sure it didn't sound like grown men.

The fighting stopped.

Every Lick that saw Ena's devastation sounded for a full retreat. Dissipating the crab, Ena felt the fatigue of ether and emotions running their course. Her limit couldn't be approaching. Not yet! Someone handed her food and she didn't even taste it. It was nourishment, pure and simple. Shivering, her body chewed to the rhythm of pounding drums.

The Black Touched were elated in victory, shouting insults to the routed Licks. Wrapped and wounded muttered, "So comes the Dawn." It almost rose up into a chant until Night silenced them.

"We shouldn't have any resistance from here on," Night told Ena. "Another half hour and we'll be in sight of Tostadt."

Someone grabbed Ena's boot. It was Fox, the burned woman with half her face black. She looked to Ena with desperation. "It's Hooper." She was pleading, pointing to Myrrel with a flailing of her arms. "Your friend can't help him. Please, you have to do something."

Ena could barely sit up in her saddle. She looked back at a mass of bodies on the floor. Blood mingled with blood and she couldn't tell the dead Licks from the injured Black. The longer she looked back at them, the more people raised their heads in hope. If she helped one, she'd move to help ten, and wouldn't have the power to destroy the balebog.

"I can't heal any more. I'm sorry," Ena told Fox.

The woman let go of Ena's boot. Her hand swung lifeless at her side. Hope died in her eyes and was replaced by nothing. Ena pulled Gale away and left Fox to mourn.

THE FIFTY-FOURTH CHAPTER

Where Ena Fights the Dead

Dark clouds hung over the balebog. Traveling clouds of white pressed up against the disk of unmoving clouds and they met in a cascade of rainfall. From a distance, it looked like something was ripping the white cloud to sunder, pulling it to the ground before it could combine with the unchanging thunder cloud. It wasn't even noon, and picturesque beams of light shone through the disk of mist. Skeletons looked like an infestation of roaches from so far away and the beams of sunlight sent them scattering. Inside the balebog, it was darker than night, but the sun reflect a rot-colored indigo off the bog's surface. Reptear structures poked up from the soil that grew no grass, their raised wooden towers protecting them from the eroding blight. Judging from the illuminated parts, Tostadt had tens of thousands of Reptear.

Night took in the sight of that horrible land and spared no time saying his goodbyes. He was scared and admitted it. No human would dare to travel into those lands.

"In Caredor, balebogs are a minor inconvenience." Myrrel was talking to the group as much as Bogelb. "Most animals have too much sense to wander into the blighted lands. So it sends out skeletons as far as they can wander. When animals come between the skeleton and the blighted land, it jumps up and spooks the animal, scaring it into the balebog. We have a saying in Caredor: 'Don't run from skeletons.' Here, they have enough skeletons to just kill anything that comes near. How can the Reptear live in there?!"

"No one knows how Reptear tame monsters," Bogelb said in apology.

"In Ki'an, battles pause to kill monsters. Both sides work as allies to kill monsters where they lie. *This* is unthinkable," Visk growled.

"Balebogs start to eat away at the soil if they don't get enough meat," Sal reminded them. "That land could be full of sinkholes."

They were scared, Ena realized. They were having these factual discussions of what they saw because they didn't want to feel anything. It was a land of darkness where maneating lizard-people worked with reanimated skeletons to kill. Fear was the rational response.

"Ena." Torno's voice brought her comfort and the sight of him was a welcome distraction from that land of darkness and death. "You're suffering from ether drain, aren't you?"

The question made her feel the fatigue in her bones. Rolling the reins in her hands, even riding felt cumbersome. "Yeah."

"How?" Myrrel asked. "She's like a living battery of ether."

"Because we trained her wrong," Torno admitted with a sigh of defeat. "Between the bleeding and her manifesting forty-foot tall monsters, her combat efficiency might be less than ten percent." He muttered, "Narla would've seen this coming."

"Torno, I was holding onto manifested ethereal creations for hours," Ena reminded him.

"Yes, but you were making them about this high." He gestured with his hands. "Besides, part of the reason we don't bleed is because the stress of battle will make ether pour out during the fighting. One sword swing in combat has the same fatigue as a hundred swings while training. It's the same idea here. Combat makes our emotions flare up, and as long as Ena taps into that, she's bleeding out more ether than entire towns produce in a day."

"Who has Narla's Monster Manual?" Myrrel asked.

"I do." Visk took it out of her pack and met inquisitive eyes.

"It helps me sleep."

Myrrel flipped through it.

"I don't really understand any of this magic talk," Bogelb admitted, "but shouldn't we go back into the city? After a night's rest she'll be ready to fight."

"The wind is blowing south now." Sal pointed to the clouds. "When it shifts to the east come nightfall, the Reptear will smell the city and all of the dead and dying. Come nightfall, they're going to swarm the city and kill everything they can carry."

"You all knew this?" Bogelb looked pale.

"We told you it was dangerous." Visk took in her fear with a grin.

"I didn't think you meant suicidal!"

Myrrel brought the conversation back to removed facts. "Caredor has never seen a balebog this big. There's nothing in here about them controlling weather. But according to the manual, a gentle shift of the earth can make the blight recede."

"Does it list the blight's entropy factor?" Ena asked.

"This has it at zero point four."

Too high to ride through miles of the blight. Ena couldn't do exact calculations in her head, but even if the ground held up, her estimate had the blight eating through Gale's hooves in about ten minutes. That dark and full cumulonimbus hung motionless in the sky. There had to be some way to use that.

"Myrrel, give Ena your wand," said Torno.

Myrrel shrugged. "I hardly use it anyway."

"Torno, I haven't been training to bleed with this. If I use the wand, I might start casting like the old Ena."

"That's what I'm counting on. You'll go back to pulling all of your punches and never running out of spells to cast. If things get bad, you'll have the bracelet and rings on your freehand. We don't have time to retrain you, so this'll have to work. For anyone else, feeling low on ether would mean we were out of options. You could still have hundreds of gulda left, maybe even a thousand. That should be more than enough for you pretending to cast like a Citadel reject. You got a plan yet, fearless leader?"

More like fearful leader. "Yes, but Sal's not going to like it."

"I like most things," he said with a joking pout.

"He and I are splitting from the group again."

"You're right. I don't like it."

~ ~ ~

Gale was happy to gallop, but the closer they got to the edge of the blight, the more skittish he became. Ena couldn't blame him. The land here had been trampled down. Nothing littered the ground, not the shed skin of Reptear, nor the droppings of animals. Reptear were gathering everything they could to feed the insatiable blight, and that meant this had to be part of their regularly traveled lands.

Sal rolled up to the edge of the blight. There was just enough sun hitting the west side of the balebog to illuminate the ground touched by it. They'd waited for this moment, for the moment when the sun shifted onto the blight. The ground was covered in a film of shimmering indigo, but underneath the dirty was crumbly dry.

Sal left his ball with a cautious slowness. He was covered in a layer of hardened clay to protect the pebbly skin between his stone scales. Drawing a winding shape in the air, Sal did his best to communicate where they needed to step. This was all guess work, anyway. None of this needed to be exact.

Taking her time to run through the basic wand forms, she recited an incantation for geomancy. The spell didn't need to be strong; it just needed to be big. That meant she had to add an the incantation for normalizing radial energy. Envision the sphere, spread out the power so it's even, flatten it to a concentrated disk, and then even it out again. Ena drew on four geometric incantations she hadn't thought about since her time in the Citadel. There was plenty of contempt for her to draw on from her time a student. She flicked a strand of yellow ether out of her wand.

Light illuminated skeletons covered in the blight. There was a deliberate way in which the skeletons had positioned themselves; about ten feet apart. The corpses lay isolated in circles roughly the size of Ena's rug. It was a chilling comparison. That strand of ether hit the ground and everything rattled. The indigo film sucked into the skeletons. It joined to their joints, pulling their spines up to bring the body erect. What film was left on the ground seemed to run from the circle of geomantic power. The skeletons stood up and looked right at her.

Ena learned a lot from that little patch of skeletons. First and foremost, they couldn't see. They had to be using some kind of geomancy to locate their prey. Those in the middle of Ena's evoked circle of power spun around in confusion, looking for the source of the disturbance. Then all at once, the skeletons walked off the circle and made their way onto the remaining blight, but they did not fall back down. Instead every skeleton sat beside their compatriots like a warrior awaiting an ambush. Ena also learned something encouraging. There were Reptear skeletons among the humans and animals.

Sal turned to look at Ena, and in that single moment two to three dozen skeletons rattled to attention. The indigo film over their mouths, spines, and joints shimmered. Ena didn't wait for them to rally. She held onto that feeling of shock and unease and sent out a directed arc of raw force.

They were deafened by bones rattling and scraping against each other. Hundreds of skeletons rose to drag Ena into the pit of decay, and there were plenty more where that came from. She moved up, following Sal to the new edge of the blight. Rapid flicks of her wand sent out small, unfocused bursts of cold that froze the balebog's film. Skeletons froze into place, forming physical walls between her and the miles of dead. Some tried to step on the frozen patches, but their bony feet could only slip and trip. Weakened bones snapped, but the blight slithered up to restore cracks and push the skeletons forward.

Casting as fast as her wrist could fly, Ena found it easy to keep her focus. She didn't need to imagine shapes or keep track of where her energy was flowing. She could cast and forget. She didn't even need to watch the blue strands of power land. They reached a new edge and Ena could cast another disk of geomancy with four flicks of her wand. The skeletons were pushing in, but as long as Ena kept freezing the edges of their path, it slowed them down enough for Ena to stay ahead. She stood up in her stirrups, focused on the growing dread in her heart, and froze skeletons.

Skeletons were working their way through the back and Ena met them with an over the shoulder cast. The bigger problem was the torches flickering on. Reptear were rising. From their raised structures the lizardfolk were easy to see. They were slow to move, though, so much slower than the ones she'd killed before. It was the lack of sun. Reptear might be magical creatures, but they were still lizards. Without sunlight to bask in they were withering to work alongside their invincible army of skeletons. All these Reptear were looking pretty thin too.

Reptear poked at the blight to rouse the skeletons around their homes. That indigo film sucked into the skeletons and left a patch of dirt for the Reptear to stand. Even still, the Reptear didn't simply walk on the ground. They'd fashioned some kind of raised sandals. Others crawled over the blight on stilts six feet long. War horns sounded and torches lit up the blight like the night's stars igniting in a wave.

Now that they were up, Ena might as well give them something to worry about.

Undirected spells tended to follow their natural motion. Flames burst up. Cold spread out and down. Water kept a shape only until it could come together in a sphere. Lightning was risky to cast when metal was around. These Reptear weren't fools. They'd gathered up metal for armor and weapons so the survivors of Hochel wouldn't have arms to fight back. Shape was an important part of any lightning spell, because without even a little bit of directed power, it would flow back at the caster. Ena wrapped a conical incantation into the spell cast from her wand. Her node? That sickening smell of the Cannegurin's mouth.

The orange bolt of ether shot straight up. Grabbing onto the strand with her bracelet, she pinched it in and bled. Holding the strand together with disgust, she watched the bolt sail half a mile straight up before popping. It was too far to direct now. The spell would only work now if she'd cast everything perfectly. She brought her attention back to the gathering skeletons and felt a satisfying shiver as thunder rumbled.

Ena slapped on her shades. Dark as the blight was, she was blind casting. But the darkness faded fast once bolts of lightning started raining down on the wooden structures. The Reptear liked weapons of war, they liked to hoard, and they liked to build with wood. Put those things together and they'd created lightning rods attached to campfires.

Narla had told Ena that she believed monsters worked on magic, that they could not only feel magic, but that magic powered them. The heart of the balebog had to control thousands of skeletons, keep back the lightning and rain, control the wind, and now it was having to recede small portions that were on fire. Like a caster overtaxed, the balebog was losing control. Rain started to fall.

"Ena!" Sal shouted. He could barely hold back his excitement.

Ena used that excitement to pull at the wind with her off hand. She wouldn't need much of a breeze to mess with the heart of the balebog. She could feel it pushing back against Ena's spell, and the more it did, the more the rain spread. "You're fucked now," she muttered.

Cold's greatest weakness was its inability to move matter. Even fire moved air around as it combusted, but cold was something hard to see. One could feel the effects of cold, but not where cold ended. Ice gave cold that edge that it needed, and now that there were years of storm clouds releasing, Ena could shape the land like a child playing in snow.

Walls of ice erected. Balls of ice the size of Sal fell down. Spikes jutted out and broke apart Reptear structures like they were piles of sticks. Javelins flew through the rain only to meet sheets of ice. The more devastation Ena threw out, the more skeletons rose, and the more the rain poured down on them. She'd stress tested the balebog and it was unraveling.

The blight pulled back to its source so fast it left patches of bone inert on the ground. It stabilized. Sal rolled forward, using his natural geomancy to sense where the ground could support them. Ena cleared the way for him with disks of geomancy. Stopping at the new, smaller circle of the blight Ena shot up another strand of lightning. The clouds stirred and again the blight pulled back for the balebog to regain control. They were physically pushing back the blight, a torrent of rain turning the balebog into a swampy graveyard. It took very little magic for Ena to create solid walls of ice between her and the Reptear.

She'd been right about the distribution of Reptear. They couldn't survive in the heart of the balebog because there was no light in the cneter. It was only her and the skeletons now, and the heart could only recede until it reached a manageable size. Once it was the size of a town or a farm, Ena wouldn't have the power to disturb it, but she didn't need to. She just needed to keep the attention of the balebog heart so Torno, Visk, and Bogelb could get Myrrel into position.

They'd been coming up from the south side of the baleblog, where the sun couldn't penetrate the dark clouds. No Reptear could live there. And since the skeletons sensed with geomancy, the same shifting that kept the blight back also kept the skeletons from seeing where they were. As long as they went slow and focused on a small disk of geomancy, they could get close enough to the heart to hit it with a deathstaff.

Ena wasn't close, maybe a mile and a half away from the center of Tostadt and the monstrous heart of the balebog. But she was close enough to see the orange strand of ether zap out the deathstaff. It popped before the heart, but stayed together as a single, solid bolt of electricity. It struck a core of blight big as a farmer's silo.

One shot was all it took. The blight unbonded and turned to mottle. The skeletons fell. And rain poured down.

"Yeah!" Ena jumped off Gale and danced in that rain. She ran up to Sal and punched his fist hard enough to hurt.

"Let's go meet up with them!" Sal shouted over the storm.

Sal led the way, turning to avoid sinkholes that were quickly turning into pits. Everywhere she looked, piles of bone were sliding into mud. The blight was a memory and those fucking Reptear couldn't do a thing about it. Visk was standing on her horse waving a red lightning-imbued spear over her head to signal them.

Ena jumped off Gale and ran up to meet them. Myrrel was soaked to the bone, Torno's deathstaff still in her hand. "I did it, Ena, did you see?!"

"I did!" She ran up and hugged her. She was wet and warm and alive. They were all okay. "I saw it, Myrrel! That was amazing!" Ena pulled back to laugh and bask in Myrrel's victory.

"You guys are bonkers!" Bogelb shouted.

"You will be, too," Ena laughed. "Just you wait!"

"I shook the ground, Ena!" Visk said. She picked Ena up and hugged her. "I did utility magic."

"I knew you could. You did great!"

Visk put her down and ran off to pick up Bogelb and spin her around. Bogelb tried to tell her to stop and then she was in the cyclone with nothing she could do about it.

Ena looked up at the rain and pulled her head back. It felt so fresh. It had years of debris to wipe clean.

"You did great, Leader," came the gruff, trying-to-be-cool voice of Torno.

She ran up and hugged him. "*We* did, Torno! You got three people to use magic like they'd never done before. I take back everything I ever said, Torno. You're a great leader."

He wasn't committing to the hug. He only had one arm on her back. He didn't share her elated grin or the ecstatic shouts of the others. He looked positively grumpy with those rivers of water rolling off his curly hair.

Ena slapped his chest. "Stop being so serious! We actually did something good for a change!"

"Yeah." It barely came out as a whisper.

She pushed her face into the taller man's chest and hugged him tight. He rested his chin on the top of her head and embraced her back; with both arms finally. He was so strong and tall and warm. She didn't want to let go of him even as the rain curled up her nose.

"What now?" Sal screamed over the roar of thunder.

"I'm too weak to kill those Reptear," Visk said.

Ena extricated herself from Torno's arms. "We'll have to ride to the closest town and get them to organize a militia."

"Why would they send an army to attack the Reptear now? They couldn't do it before," Myrrel asked.

"Because those Reptear are malnourished. They couldn't kill a teenager with a cold. There's nothing alive within miles of this place and if I had to guess they've been eating each other. Their whole plan was doomed to fail. All it needed was for someone to come in and give them a little poke, and we did it." Ena turned her head back to the sky. "We did it!"

THE FIFTY-FIFTH CHAPTER

In Which Heartbeats Slow

Humans riding out of the city of the dead was cause for curiosity. Wall fortifications opened up and half the town of Alba Numa came out to meet the strangers who'd survived an army of Reptear. Guards stepped to the front not with suspicion, but to keep order. Everyone had questions. The children kept looking around for a short Leben boy with a Turall marked heater shield, but no matter how many asked if they could see Muttur, there was only Ena. Still, the guards kept order, and a matter this important needed to go straight to the Leutemast, Erchritt's equivalent to a Sorcerer. Every able body crowded around the steps of the Leutemast's Quarters but celebratory highs were made weary by the lie Ena needed to tell.

"We were leaving Hochel, and saw the clouds moving away from Tostadt."

One lie lead to others and the people were skittish, suddenly guarded by the words of these strangers, Leben, Gulam, Ki'an, and Boulba all moving together with unknown purpose. Bogelb did her best to rally the people to action, to convince them that the Reptear were emaciated and vulnerable, but they wouldn't rouse to action. So it was that Ena gave a rallying speech in a language she barely spoke.

"*Reptear killed family. Reptear ate family. Reptear killed all food. Reptear grow weak. Reptear eat Reptear! Reptear grow weaker! Time to kill is now! Twenty kill one hundred! Fifty kill a thousand! Go! Get your weapons! Unite and kill them all! Take back your land!*"

As she spoke, lashes of curious empathic spells kept

brushing against her. The Leben trusted her empathy more than her words or even her voice. Ena remembered the dead children of the Black who had fought to put an end to these Reptear. She pushed out the feelings of anticipation leading into that battle, the need to end evil and protect the people she loved. Those feelings at last swayed them.

Some village hero spoke up in support of Ena's speech and skepticism at last gave way to inhibition. A mother of three who had been a mother of seven announced her decision to join and avenge her husband and sons. Courage gave rise to courage, and soon hundreds were marching off to kill the Reptear.

But Team Freedom was exhausted.

In a mostly empty tavern, they rested their minds with quiet gawking, drinking to ease the last of their adrenaline to sleep. People were out fighting. There would be deaths, Ena knew, but those Reptear would break before the spirit of a people who'd faced undead hordes for years without any chance to strike back. It would be a good day for Alba Numa.

"You are incredible." Sal raised his mug of oil. "It's going to be amazing watching you lead all of Doronel."

"Hey, cut that out!" Ena slapped his arm. "I'm not leading anyone."

"Are you kidding me?!" snorted Bogelb. "You basically got this town to ride off to war with baby talk. Leading people is your destiny. We should all be drinking to *you*!"

Ena waved the idea away and physically lowered mugs when they were raised. "No, no, no. Stop that! This isn't about me. We did this. This was a team effort and none of us could've made it without every single person here."

"We couldn't have done it without Narla," Torno added seriously. "It was her knowledge of monsters and magic that gave us what we needed to win. To Narla."

Ena had no objections to that toast, and she drank until she suppressed a choke to honor her. Her mug was last to slam down, but she slammed it with as much gusto as Narla would've.

"What's the plan now?" asked Bogelb.

No one in the bar was paying any attention to them. The lone bartender was a girl of fourteen caught up in a conversation with two other girls around her age. "We continue to the treasury, but there's a good chance he's from this region. If we keep asking around, we might find his hometown. Talking to the people who grew up with him could give us some insight into how he thinks."

"And then you're going to use that to kill him." The idea still unsettled Bogelb.

Ena tried to handle this diplomatically. "We'll go to Doronel before engaging him directly. How far are you planning on going with us, Bogelb?"

"I don't know," she admitted. "After today, I'm not sure. Do any of you think we'll see Vamere again?"

Myrrel shook her head. "Vamere seemed beyond saving to me."

Visk snorted. "Why *would* we save him?"

Talk of Vamere was only going to bring the mood down. Ena raised her hands and chuckled. "Hey, we can worry about that later. Tonight is about celebrating. I hope you're all ready to be embarrassed, because we are going to celebrate each and every one of you tonight."

Ena went around the table and made sure each of them spoke about how important they were to each other. It was awkward for Bogelb, since they were still getting to know her, but she got along with the group. To Ena, Bogelb was more than a guide, she was quickly becoming a friend.

The whole time Ena was dreading saying nice things about Torno. She wanted to ramble on endlessly about how important he was to her. Complicating things was having him be last at the queue, with his body beside her. That rank musk of him was adding heat to anticipation, making it all wickedly pleasant. Yeah, talking about him might get weird.

When the time finally came for Ena to make a speech about Torno, the tavern door opened. A haggard man red with blood gave the news, the wounded were returning. They needed all available hands to tend the wounded. Of course, that prideful fool with an endless summer scent rose to help them. Torno was out of magic, but he knew enough medicine to help with nothing but his hands. Ena followed him without hesitation.

Drunk and full of thoughts of trying to steal Torno away for herself, Ena followed direction like a child given their first shot at heroism—earnest, but lacking initiative or sense. Physically Ena was next to useless, but she wrapped wounds and applied pressure as Visk ordered. Just as the injured felt managed, a caravan returned from the fighting. An older man with a salt and pepper beard was lowered on a gurney. His son was at his side, and he wouldn't let go of his hand. This man was going to die.

Myrrel put her hand on Ena's shoulder. "I know that look."

"I can't let him die, Myrrel." Ena washed her hands with speed. She wished there was a spell to sober her up.

"I know, Ena. I'm going to go in there with my hands and you're going to use magic when and how I say, do you understand?"

She nodded.

"But you have to be ready for him to die."

Myrrel was in control. No matter what happened, she was focused. Myrrel performed triage while operating and lead Ena to dab at blood and magically seal veins. This was the reason Ena had always seen Myrrel haggard and disheveled. The woman cared so much about helping people. But it wasn't more than her innate compassion that kept her working. Strange as it was, Myrrel was at peace there. Healing people was her calling. She knew what needed to be done and she never second guessed herself. She accepted every death with dignity and never lingered on a life that she saved. Ena did her best to mirror Myrrel's confidence. Under her guidance they performed magic that she'd never before tried and they saved that boy's father. Ena waited around to see that look of relief in that scared teen's eyes. Myrrel tossed aside Ena's bloody wig and moved on to save another.

~ ~ ~

Visk was carrying Ena like a baby. Ena met her eyes and then nuzzled into her arms.

"Having a good time, my child?"

"Mmhmm," Ena cooed happily.

She chuckled. "That's good. I was a little worried you might go into another ether coma."

"I'm just a little drunk is all." It was a good thing Visk was carrying her, because Ena didn't like the idea of walking. "I'm very drunk and very tired."

"We're almost back at the inn."

"Did we save everyone?"

"We saved many people," Visk told her. "We spent too much magic saving the Blacks, and then we saved the region destroying the city of the dead, and then we saved people with our bare hands. I can't believe you let Torno run off to heal people and I can't believe I joined you."

"Why didn't Torno carry me back?"

"Because the fool did what you did," Visk chuckled. "He might be out for days. He cannot stand to watch a woman die."

"I love him," Ena told Visk.

"I know." She readjusted Ena in her arms. "I'm going to stand you up now. Can you lean against me?"

Ena made a sound that was supposed to be confirming. Standing was bad. No person that ever existed should stand. Crawling was natural. All things crawled but very few stood. Sitting on the floor felt right while drunk.

"Making me do everything the hard way, are we?" Visk said in good spirits. She picked up Ena.

Ena used her legs to steady herself. She followed Visk's legs, trying to crab walk to keep up with the woman's long stride. Luckily, the bed was close. That soft sweet bed welcomed Ena. Visk pulled at her jacket.

"Visk, I meant what I said about Torno. I love him."

Visk let Ena go and she fell back into the pillows. The door shut.

"Yes, I told you I know," Visk whispered. "His room is close to yours."

"Am I being loud?"

"You are screaming in my ear, yes."

Ena gurgled something that was supposed to be an apology.

Visk stroked Ena's face. She'd gotten most of her clothes off.

"Visk, I have to tell you about Torno," she whispered.

Visk chuckled. "You just did."

"I did?"

"You spent the last half hour telling me about how you fell in love with him as a little girl," Visk explained. "It is sweet and a little scary."

"Love is scary."

Visk looked down with pained sympathy. "Yes, it is."

"You...it...you'll find love again, Visk."

"I don't know if I can," she admitted. "I think Bogelb might like me, but she is young. I would have to teach her too much."

"What if you don't fall in love with her?" Ena giggled and tried to reach up to kiss Visk.

Visk kept Ena down with a single finger on her forehead.

Ena ceased her struggle. "Kiss her and see what happens."

"That is not my way, Ena. I love with my entire body." Fear was a storm thundering up from Visk's lungs.

"Visk, do you think I should tell Torno how I feel?"

"I don't know," she admitted. "He has been a great many things to you and enemy was one of them. When the two of you fight you will have a great many things to yell at each other."

"Did you fight with Duli?"

Thinking of her dead lover brought a fond smile to Visk's lips. "Many times." She kissed Ena's forehead. "Now rest."

~ ~ ~

Puking helped Ena fight her hangover, and so did eating pickles, sausage, and eggs, but it still irked. Everyone else was fine. It made Ena feel like a little girl to be the only person hungover. The town had gathered to give this big celebration and she wanted no part of it. They dragged her out of the inn to hear kind words and receive gifts, but Ena beat them all by dragging out a bed sheet. She wrapped it around her head to block out the light and the sounds. They laughed at her and Bogelb made her shake people's hands. But soon she was climbing on Gale and riding away from the people of Alba Numa.

This was what all this struggling was for. These people were alive. They were wounded and bandaged, but they were hopeful. Tomorrow would be good because they could once again have control over their lives. Killing the weakened Reptear had only been the beginning. They still had a lot of work ahead of them, but they weren't afraid of the challenge. Ena needed to hold onto that moment. This was what the Gods were denying with their Grand Dream. They were keeping people from forging their own futures.

"*Be sad!*" She told them. "*Be strong, be brave, and be sad!*"

She thought they would laugh, they'd been laughing at her for almost an hour, but her simple words were enough for the mourning to nod with understanding. They wished her luck on her journey with a wave. Ena hadn't been wearing her blue skin cream that entire morning, but they didn't care. Or if they did, no one said word one about Ngoltur.

~ ~ ~

They reached a village hours from the treasury at nightfall. The small place wasn't on the map and there was a strange energy to it besides. The locals were aggressive, staring daggers at them from the edge of the city. A child yelled, "*Go away!*" Her mother pulled the girl back muttering something about weapons. Ena looked at the deathstaff and sword showing on Torno's schistrau and the spear on Visk's back. They did not look like friendly strangers.

Bogelb ran up to ask their questions, but an older woman was already yelling something snippy at them.

"She says that they don't want any foreigners around. That man runs a market and will let us trade for goods," Bogelb translated. More were talking, some argued aggressive enough to pull at threads.

Ena asked Torno, "Do you still have that drawing of Muttur you made?"

He got it out.

"Lady," came the voice of an old Gulam man. He spoke in passable Dorospek. "Do not speak of prophecy."

"Sorry." Ena bowed her head. "Is the Leutemast here?"

Heads looked around and none found him. But the crowd was now twenty people strong standing tall in the coming drizzle.

"Here," Torno handed over the picture.

Ena took shelter under an awning, passing the picture to the old Gulam man. "Have you seen this boy?"

The vocal old woman snatched it out of Ena's hands. She riled the crowd up to a frenzy with a single word. Passing the picture around as they smacked his likeness. "Bogelb?"

"They're calling him Run-boy. They're speaking curses."

Myrrel was shocked and a little relieved. "They don't like him?" They were all dismounted now.

"They're calling him bastard and kikaa shit. It's safe to say they hate him," Bogelb explained.

"*He kill friend*," Ena yelled over them. "*We hunt him!*"

Their suspicious anger turned to solid approval. Still others regarded Ena with pity; they knew in their hearts that she would die in the attempt. Team Freedom was led to a place they called *The Big House*. There they met the Leutemast and listened to the shared story of Muttur's arrival.

THE FIFTY-SIXTH CHAPTER

In Which the Nature of
Muttur is Revealed

Muttur galloped into town. He didn't lead his schistrau in on a trot or canter, he rode the schistrau at a hard gallop. He jumped off the back of the schistrau and just let it keep galloping forward. Then the boy ran straight to the market. Not at a jog, he sprinted to the marketplace. Once he inside, he ran right past a customer chatting up the owner and flung a bag onto the table. Inside were flowers, weeds, insects, bones, and Reptear skins. He pointed at them and made a shouting sound that was almost a question. With nothing but gestures the boy got them to understand he was trying to sell them this garbage.

The merchant was moving things around, showing that this was worthless and the boy's shouts got angrier. He smelled bad, like body odor and an open pond. He was roughed up and had obviously been on the road for a long time, so out of sense of pity, the merchant cater to his demands. The customer left to find the kid some help, but Run-boy wandered into the back of the store.

The merchant's son was back there, a boy of eight. Run-boy stared at him until the kid asked, "What are you doing here?" Then he ignored the kid and ran through the house connected to the store. He opened every door, checked every room, went through every closet, and opened every dresser and box that he could. When one of the boxes was locked, he smashed it into a wall to open it. Then he rummaged around the contents and took nothing.

All of this commotion brought the merchant back, but Run-boy ignored all his demands to stop. He just ran past him. Whatever money was still on the counter, he swiped and ran outside.

By this point, three men were waiting outside to help the boy settle down and talk. Run-boy ignored them to a man, jogging to get to the next place. But then one of them called out to him and he stopped. He went perfectly still and faced them with his shoulders squared. They tried to explain that he was scaring people but he didn't react. When they asked if he was going to cause any more trouble, he gave a single smiling nod and took off into a sprint.

That was when Run-boy's behavior got even weirder.

First of all, the kid didn't care about his schistrau—at all. He didn't take the schistrau to be stabled. He didn't even look at the thing. He just ran around town. He ran down every street, went into every house and searched every room. Occasionally, he would stop before someone and stare at them. He would stare at people with a vacant expression until they said something. It didn't matter what they said, once they finished talking, he would break into a jog and continue searching the entire town.

He tossed every jar and pot he could find, sifting through the debris to find anything of value inside. He pocketed coins and anything else he thought he could sell. Any barrels or boxes that happened to be lying in the street, he smashed them open. He ruined four barrels of wine by hacking them open with a simple traveler's sword.

After busting up the supplies outside the tavern, Run-boy went inside and ordered food like nothing had happened. He shoveled it into his mouth, finishing baked apples in three bites and kikaa thighs in five. The tavern owner told him to leave and just like before he stopped eating to listen. The second the owner was done yelling at him, Run-boy left. So the people he'd robbed got together and told him to leave, one after another.

Dutifully, patient as a statue he stood and listened. During all this commotion, six people had the bright idea to get together and form a militia to force him out.

That's when Run-boy got violent. The moment blades were drawn, he rushed at them. He dodged every blow and rushed in to cut the attackers down. The moment his sword struck flesh he hack at them until their bodies hit the ground. One man he stabbed in the neck, and even though he was clearly dead, Run-boy kicked at his back to keep him from falling. He struck at the lifeless body three more times before it hit the ground. He killed the six of them and four more that took up arms. No a one of them landed a single blow.

Those gathered outside ran. They locked their doors, boarded up their windows, and watched with horror.

Run-boy ransacked the body of every person he killed, sifting through their pockets and coin pouches. Then he just continued his search. He kept running through the entire town. When he'd checked every street, he started shaking doors to make sure they were locked. But even after he'd tried every door, he wasn't done. Run-boy climbed onto roofs, jumping from building to building to see if there was anything worth keeping. At some point he tried to jump over an alley and fell down. That should've been it. No boy could survive a fall like that. He fell two stories and landed on his back, but it didn't phase him. Run-boy grunted and got right back up. He tried to make the jump two more times before he started trying all the windows to get up on that roof.

Frustrated, he chopped the door down. The fletcher was inside, hiding behind the counter. Run-boy went shopping. He grabbed a quiver, about twenty arrows, a bow, and slapped them onto the table. Covered in blood, the boy paid for the bow and arrows with coins he'd gotten from the fletcher's recently murdered friends. There was this creepy, meaningless smile on his face when the shaking fletcher thanked the boy for his business.

Another strangeness about Run-boy was that he didn't

have any feelings. People kept reaching out to feel his emotions, but there was nothing there. He wasn't happy when he smiled. He wasn't angry when he screamed and cut people down. He was moving but he didn't feel anything. It was like Run-boy was a doll of flesh who lived to collect money.

Once he had the bow and arrows he left. But he didn't leave on the schistrau he came in on. Instead, he ran over to the schistrau in the stables and proceeded to test each and every one of them. He'd jump on, ride it about twenty strides and back before moving on to try the next bird. He checked every single schistrau before stealing his favorite and riding it into the woods.

That wasn't the end of it.

Two days later, there was this pounding sound, like the striking of thunder. They'd never heard anything like it. Eight men got together to check it out, and they left with shields and armor. Muttur was the source of that sound. He was smashing into trees. He would shake his feet on the ground and the winged boots would propel him forward like an arrow. He slammed into trees and looked to see if anything fell. He'd cracked probably a hundred trees that way and broken another hundred.

One of the men who had seen Muttur fight had gone to investigate. The sight of Run-boy froze him. He found a bush to hide in and curled up into a ball, but the others tried to surround and kill him. It was the same as before. He'd cut someone until they hit the ground. His sword bent and he grabbed one from the dead. He never missed an arrow shot and every slash connected with its target. Run-boy hadn't even parried a single attack. He only dodged and killed.

When Run-boy saw the lone survivor, he stood over him until he begged the boy, "Don't kill me." Then he just shifted his feet, flew off, and sprinted back to the village.

Run-boy ran straight to the marketplace and hefted his bag of junk onto the counter. This time the merchant gave him every coin he had, but it was no different. Run-boy took the money with a lifeless smile.

Back he went to the stable, and same as before, he checked the speed of every schitrau. Some stable kid had missed the excitement the last time he was around. Thinking him a new assistant, he challenged Run-boy to a race. With a smile and a nod, Run-boy accepted. They bet five silver a race, and the kid won. Run-boy didn't quibble. He didn't argue or attack the stablehand, he simply got another schistrau until he found the fastest.

This was when the angry woman got involved. Her husband had been among the men that fought Run-boy the first time around. She walked up to chew him out, yelling everything she could possibly think at him. But he didn't react at all, no matter what she said, he just stood there with that same lifeless smile. Her words meant nothing to him; not her pain, not her anger, not her words of judgment. During the entire lecture, he smiled and waited for her to finish. Frustrated she asked, "Don't you have anything to say for yourself?"

His response was ride off, going north-east towards Karzak.

That was the last any had seen of him.

~ ~ ~

Ena was stunned to silence. She'd never heard of anyone acting like so erratic. It was one thing to be motivated by money, but why search through pots and boxes for forgotten bits of change and junk? If he was that desperate for coin, he could just kill the people and take their stuff. For that matter, why pay for a bow and arrow when the fletcher had been cowering behind his counter? She couldn't make sense of his motivations.

"They want to know if you think you can kill him?" Bogelb asked.

"Do they know how Run-boy got the winged-boots?" Ena asked.

She shook her head.

Ena swore a vow to the widows. "I will kill him. If I have to follow him to the far lands, I will kill him."

Bogelb translated and that seemed to settle them.

It was so late. Between the tears and the outpours of emotion to go with their explanations, Ena was exhausted. She got up to leave and that old Gulam man spoke up.

"Why did you call him Muttur?"

They all knew that word, and when he spoke it the people analyzed Ena in a different light. The truth would shake up everything they believed. Muttur was more than a myth to the people of Leben Erde, he was practically a god.

"I was mistaken," Ena told him.

The old man didn't believe her. She could see it in his eyes, but what did it matter?

They left the Big House and walked to the inn under pattering rain.

"What are we going to do?" asked Myrrel.

"They said he came from down the road. We should be able to track his path of destruction back to his home town. There's gotta be a reason he's like that. Maybe someone used imperfect empathy magic on him and it messed up his brain," Ena grumbled. She was so tired.

"What I mean was, what are we going to do about Runboy? You heard how they talked about how he fought. He didn't waste a single stroke. He only attacked to kill and he never missed," she said with fear. Myrrel had known what his attacks were like when an arrow hit her in the throat.

"He didn't kill you." Ena stopped to talk. The parched Bogelb continued on to the inn. Ena made no effort to stop her. "Listen, strong as he might be, Muttur is human."

"What if he isn't?" Torno asked. "I shot him with my deathstaff. It hit him straight on. An attack like that should've burned his flesh off. It didn't even singe his clothes."

"I know," Ena rubbed her tired eyes. She walked under the awning of the inn to get out of the rain. "It could be some kind of personal protection field, like what Hultur had."

"He was also running everywhere. I have never known

magic to remove fatigue." Visk looked to Myrrel.

She shook her head. "Me neither. Maybe Hultur could explain it, but it sounds impossible to me."

"What if the Gods favor him?" Sal asked. "Muttur has always come last. Ngoltur surrenders, Hultur is killed, but Muttur is never defeated. I can't think of a single cycle of the Grand Dream where he even gets a serious injury."

"We can't think like that," Ena told them. "Magic always has limitations. Bodies need food, he probably needs to sleep. The Grand Dreamer said that she that in some timelines he is killed. We can't give up hope."

"But if we don't beat him to Vytur Castle, he takes over the world," said Torno.

"Yeah," Ena sighed. "We need to learn as much as we can about his past. If this is him as a fifteen-year-old, we can't afford to find out what he'll be as a ruler."

~ ~ ~

Following the footsteps of Muttur was chilling. People looked to Team Freedom with suspicion but shared stories that seemed to contradict the shape of his personality at every turn. If these stories described a boy that simply loved to murder, Ena would've had them go back to Schlabaum after a day. But the stories described a thing that seemed to follow a logic all of its own.

In one village, Muttur had been received with kindness. The owner of an eatery saw this dirty child run down a squirrel and eat it raw. The woman offered to feed him if he bathed and he dove into a trough and smiled at her. So she dragged him by the arm and wash herself without any escalation of violence. Back at her establishment, eating with half the people in town, he overheard a woman of nineteen mention that she lost her locket out in the fields. Run-boy ran off, stole a scythe, and cut cut down the entire field to find her locket. When he gave it to her, he wouldn't leave until someone paid him a silver. Then the thief inside him came out, breaking boxes and ransacking the village.

Strange as his behavior was, his violence was usually provoked. Sure, his responses were nowhere near proportionate but he wasn't killing simply for the thrill of it. In one instance, an orphaned girl came across Run-boy while traveling with her father. They were escaping a rash of Reptear that had burned their home. Her father was hoping to rally a rescue party for his wife. Run-boy spooked the cattle-drawn cart and her father swore at him. He responded by murdering the man and butchering his cow. It looked like he was going to kill the girl until she covered her mouth. Muttur stole every coin they had and ran off with as much meat as he could carry, which he sold to the next village over.

As they continued to travel down the road, some began to seek out Team Freedom to tell a different story about Run-boy. A honey salesman got a wheel stuck in the mud and Run-boy helped for a silver. Some newlyweds were traveling with their family and ran into Reptear on the road. Run-boy killed the Reptear and didn't even stop for a reward. Another voice of dissension came from an older man who'd recently lost his mill. He was begging in the street and Muttur helped him walk into a diner before paying for his meal. A fifteen-year-old boy saw Muttur chowing down food fast and challenged him to an eating contest.

These conflicting opinions came to a head when they reached a village that he saved from a rash of Reptear. Forty of them came in to sack the village when in ran little Run-boy. He cut through the Reptear, using the weapons of the fallen as he slayed. When the villagers bathed him to show their thanks, there wasn't a single cut on him, despite the fact that several had seen him take an arrow in the head and a spear to the gut. Everyone celebrated his heroics, but when the very next day he ransacked the town he'd just saved.

Only one person died during his trip to that village.

The wife of the deceased explained that she was talking to

her husband when he ran up and stabbed him three times, each strike fatal, and then ran off. She was beside herself with grief and had to be shown out of the room. Yet, once she was gone, several witnesses confirmed that the husband had been beating his wife that very night. They were outside because her husband had grabbed her arm to yell at her. Ena had seen those kinds of relationships herself and far too often the wife would go to extreme measures to hide the abuse. That could've been a case of Muttur seeing himself as a hero.

Several villagers asked the same question over and over again, with reverence pouring out, "Do you think he could be Muttur Reborn?"

THE FIFTY-SEVENTH CHAPTER

In Which Ena Traces the Smoke
Back to the Flames

Autumn began with daily rains in Erchritt. Ena saddled up with a stick of smoked meat in her mouth. A small procession stood outside a tavern, the storytellers wishing them luck. Much of this village saw him as a confused child that they wanted to help. But there was no confusion in his actions when he killed Narla. They hadn't antagonized him. He'd baited Ena to lower her guard and Narla paid the consequences. Ena raised her hood to protect her black wig and rode into the drizzle.

"That was something," Myrrel commented. "Since we're going backwards, it seems like he was getting better as he went on. I keep having to remind myself that it's the opposite."

"Let's ground up and discuss. Keep slow so Sal can talk," Ena kept her tone conversational.

"I can jog at this pace." Sal set the speed; his hands used for motion along with his kneeless legs. "I don't think my opinion of the killer has gotten any kinder."

"No," Torno agreed. "I don't even think he got worse as he traveled. I think that the situations were different."

"How do you mean?" Myrrel asked.

"He arrived as this village was being attacked by Reptear. Coincidences like that could be the work of the Gods."

"I thought you still believed that the Gods didn't exist," Ena teased with a raised brow.

"Something chooses the Turall. There's too many signs of their influence."

"Bogelb, what's your opinion of Muttur?"

"It's complicated." She kept her lips thin and straight as a line.

"Be honest with us," Visk urged.

Bogelb took her time to gather her thoughts before continuing. "Every Leben boy dreams that they'll one day grow up into Muttur. We play out the Grand Dream as children. When it's two of us, we'll play Muttur kills Hultur or Muttur saves Ngoltur. If twenty kids are out, we play games to decide who gets to be the Turall and who has to play a Sage. We hear about The Grand Dream with the festivals of seasons. We wish our dead well with a saying that basically means, 'may you drink with the Gods.' The Grand Dream isn't history or a story to us, it's part of who we are as a people.

"I literally can't imagine what it would be like to suddenly *be* Muttur. He has to be mute or deaf, because I can't imagine someone being Muttur and not bragging about it at least a little. From the sound of it he's *Inomercherz*, a person who can't use magic. I don't know the word for it in Dorospek."

"Ether Quorin," Torno told her. "Do all people with Ether Quorin have no emotions in Leben?"

"We don't think so, we just think we can't sense what they're feeling. Our village had a man in his mid-thirties with *Inomercherz*. He was kind and always smiled and tried to help people, but it was hard to talk to him. Most adults avoided him. Mine never minded since so much of my family was connected to Gulam, we were used to people that didn't send empathy when they talked."

"Is it hard to talk to us?" Sal asked.

"It's different." Bogelb struggled to find the words to describe it. "I've been told by boulba that it's hard to talk to humans because we don't talk with geomancy, so you must have some idea of what I'm talking about, right?"

Sal shook his head and grew dour.

"Bogelb, did you dream of being Muttur when you were a kid?" Myrrel asked conversationally.

"Umm..." Her cheeks blushed indigo. "I was a little taller than the others, so I got to play as Hultur."

Ena noticed the use of "got to," which implied that it was something she wanted to do. "Bogelb, do you think you could talk with me like Leben talk? Just the two of us."

"Yeah, for sure. Empathy magic has gotten easier for you, right?"

Ena nodded. "It requires very little conscious thought. It's kind of the opposite of Gulam magic."

"It was the same way with my sister-in-law," Bogelb assured her. "Once she let go of trying to think of magic, she didn't have any trouble casting. I wish it was as easy to learn Gulam magic, I couldn't even learn a wind spell."

"That makes perfect sense," Ena assured her. She looked over at Torno and teased him by saying, "Only the cruel are good at wind magic."

Torno rolled his eyes.

Visk was oblivious to this exchange and said, "Each person attunes easier to a different elemental focus."

"Do you think you could teach me magic in the Ki'an ways?" Bogelb asked.

Visk took a long time considering it. "We would need to wake early and sleep late to prep your body."

"Sleep don't like me already. What if we combined watches on the road, used that for training?"

Visk agreed to that with a solemn nod.

Ena wondered if she was blushing. Visk said that she thought Bogelb was romantically interested, but Ena was sure Visk was the one who was interested in her. Bogelb was a plain-looking woman, but many of her features were elongated and athletic like Visk's. When she was deep in thought she had an almost masculine charm to her and was tall besides. She was tall as Torno, which had to mean she was about six-two. That couldn't be big for Visk. She was used to women reaching her seven-one with ease, but so many Leben were short as Ena and many were even shorter.

With a lull in the conversation, Sal rolled into a ball and they rode in earnest.

Wayward thoughts of romance brought Ena's mind back to the Torno Problem. She'd been watching him ride when she thought he wasn't looking. He was so handsome it hurt Ena's heart to stare, but the second she looked away she wanted nothing more than to steal another glance. It was getting hard for Ena to convince herself that he still wanted to be with her.

Back when they were Brokers, he wouldn't stop staring at her. She'd glance back and find him looking. Calling him out on his behavior only ever got them into another one of their fights that went nowhere. Now that things were reversed, Torno didn't seem to notice Ena staring. He was nothing but professional with her, answering questions before going off to do his own thing. After years of telling him to back off and leave her alone, and it hurt her heart to have him act so damn casual!

Thought of Torno were keeping her up at night. She almost *really* thought about him, but she couldn't. It felt like a betrayal to masturbate about a man that was her friend. As a teenage girl, he'd almost been a concept. Torno, the sexy high-class man. Torno, the pained poet. Torno, the sensual lover. She'd been able to touch herself about him then, but not since meeting him. Wondering about his nightly thoughts only made everything worse. He claimed his undying crush on Ena was an honest expression of love.

She fantasized about visiting him at the inn at night; finding him and that glorious dick out. He'd try to cover up and she would magic the sheets away so he couldn't hide. And he'd be naked before her. She'd snap her fingers to burn her clothes off and...the thoughts died. Anything more would be a kind of betrayal. Or maybe it was an outcome that Ena wouldn't let herself dream because she didn't want reality to disappoint her. No, she remembered every moment of that dreamcast. Torno wouldn't disappoint her. She'd be the one to disappoint him. He'd waited years for her and Ena had only been with four people. He could be her fifth.

She wanted him to be her last.

~ ~ ~

The last stop of the day was a proper town. No one recognized Torno's second picture of Run-boy. If they were going to find out more about Run-boy, it was going to take a little bit of snooping. Ena got the sneaky idea of splitting off in pairs. Then Myrrel of all people took the initiative and paired up with Torno! It was annoying, but as long as Ena traveled the town with Sal, Visk and Bogelb would get that alone time they needed for something to happen. An hour into their search, Ena was ready to give up, but Sal wanted to check out the north side of town.

Past the edge of the north side, new growth littered the floor. What trees remained were red and black from their bark set ablaze. Destruction went on for miles to the north and by the looks of the deep trenches, the town had fought hard to keep the conflagration from climbing the stone wall. Locals said the forest fire came on fast, a kid from out of town was running from his life. Or so they thought. A guard identified Run-boy as the kid evading the blaze.

Team Freedom met at a tavern called The Drunk Schistrau. It might've been the third tavern the visited with the same name. A bartender talked up a whiskey flavored with mint and honey and Ena downed two of them within an hour. Muttur had been in the tavern the night of the blaze. A regular remembered him because he'd been to the schistrau races the night before and lost a good deal of money. Other than that, no one knew anything about the kid.

Another soft lead was discouraging, but Torno was looking delicious with those brooding eyes fixed on his drink.

Sauntering over, she bumped into his long legs while ordering a drink. "Excuse you."

"Sorry." He shifted away, downed his drink, and stood.

"I'm calling it a night."

It was annoying, but what could she do, force him to stay behind and dance? Defeated again Ena sank into the bar and passed time sipping her third mint whiskey. And it suddenly hit her how silly she was being. This was her chance. He was alone, everyone was chilling at the tavern. If she ran to the inn, she might still catch him. She might even catch him with his pants off.

"Hey," said Bogelb. "Do you want to chat?"

Ena looked to the door, but there was no sign of Torno; he'd been gone for over ten minutes. If she gave Bogelb the drink and ran after him, everyone would know what Ena was up to, and if she lost her nerve again, she'd have to live with the embarrassment of being exposed. This was bad timing. Again.

"Okay." Ena settled. "You mean talk like the Leben do, right?"

Bogelb pressed excitement into Ena's tummy. "That's right."

Ena sent out nervousness. "Here?"

"We chat back at the inn." Bogelb offered with a brush of assurance.

Ena tried to send out the feeling of shaking her head.

Bogelb shook her head. "Softer. Don't overthink it. What were you trying to send?"

"No."

Bogelb laughed. "I've heard old married couples can do that."

"Hey, Pretty," came the voice of a man who came up to Bogelb's shoulder. "Can I buy you a drink?" He licked at Ena with a glance of lust.

Ena sent out disgust. "I'm alright."

"No, thank you."

He scowled at Ena but smiled politely at Bogelb and left.

"What did you send to him?"

"Disgust?"

"No, send it like you sent to him."

Ena thought about his wet lips, slicked back hair, and crooked brows and the disgust was easy to manifest.

"Wow!" Bogelb chuckled. "That's like a *slap* of disgust. Did he really gross you out that much?"

She shrugged. "He just kind of annoyed me."

"So send that. This isn't a battle. You don't need to overpower him and you don't need to exaggerate."

Ena deflated. "I thought I was better at this."

"Don't get into your head about it. The more you think about it, the less effective you're going to be." Bogelb looked around the bar. "Why don't we go to that empty booth and talk?"

There was such a gentle feeling of confidence seeping off Bogelb. She took to this so naturally. Ena had forgotten that the woman was a year older than her. For some reason, her being nearly a foot taller than Ena wasn't enough to pound that fact into her mind. Being a Turall was screwing with her sense of time, her sense of her own age.

"What do you want to talk about?" Bogelb asked.

"Love." Ena shook the air with apprehension.

"Oh." Sorrow.

Ena sent curiosity, but then thought better and tried to send out sympathy. "What happened?"

"That first push was fine but try not to think about the emotion you send." Bogelb sent out sorrow in jagged planes of metal. "Otherwise it can come out like this."

"There's like a..." Ena waved her hand to try and find the thought. "Shape to it."

"That's a good way to put it." She sent out regret.

"So what happened?"

"Um...part of the reason I left Schlabaum was because of my feelings for Grou." Shame. "I really liked her, but I knew better than to tell her how I felt."

"Because she was younger?"

Bogelb blushed but sent shock. "Do you think four years is a lot?!"

"It can be," Ena frowned. She tried to send the feel of a

hand patting her back. "I didn't really get to know Grou. Is she mature?"

"Very. She knows a lot about people. You could send her nothing and she'd know everything you were thinking. No, it's just..." Bogelb scooted forward to whisper. "Women aren't supposed to like women here."

Ena sent annoyance.

"Torno told me Caredor doesn't have any books of fiction?"

Ena shook her head. "We have playwrights. I read a few plays last winter. One of them had never even been performed."

"These are more than people talking. They have descriptions written out in great detail. Anyway, there are some popular books in Erchritt about men who love each other. Apparently, a lot of men in Fieta have what they call war-love. Two men will love each other as long as they're fighting or in the same mercenary company, but they'll split up when they put down their swords."

"Like Ki'an women." Ena sent a flash of interest.

Lust. "They're really raunchy. It's how I came to be friends with Anior. I think he might've suspected that I liked women, but he never said anything. Even though it's becoming fashionable for men to kiss, it's not something that's taken seriously." Bogelb pointed out two men dancing. Their friends were laughing themselves indigo. "The two of them aren't actually interested in each other. The guy with the red streaks is trying to get the attention of that woman with the flower in her hair."

"Oh." Ena never would've guessed that from watching the two of them. The shorter man with a mustache seemed so passionate about the man he danced with. But after they bowed he returned to the table and gave his girlfriend a passionate kiss. She was aroused and melted into his lips. "Is it a dance of seduction?"

"I guess it is, but it's not for each other. It's kind of like a shared performance. Anior started things with that gem cutter just like that. It was all a joke, until it wasn't. Women..." Bogelb sent out something like depression. It was certainly hopeless enough to be in a situation like that. "Women don't have anything like that. Oh, sorry. Did was that feeling too complex?"

"I'll try to pick it up as we go. Do you think Grou likes you back?"

Bogelb let out a long sigh, sharing a tremor of indecision. "Last we talked, Grou didn't want anything to do with romance. She wanted to have a safe, normal life away from her perverted brother-in-law. My guess is that the first halfway decent man that catches her attention will propose within the year. She's so gorgeous."

Ena tried to send her feelings for Torno, she hoped they came off as hopeful. "What about now?"

Bogelb scanned Team Freedom and a sludge of hesitation trickled out of her. "It's not something I'm thinking about."

So Ena decided to talk about the Great Generation. She told her about the Supreme Magus's plan to make a ruling class with large wells of ether, the way dreamcasts built up the myth around them, and how people paid a lot of money for Romantic Escapes. Then, slowly, painfully, Ena told her about Torno and Kalta. When Team Freedom came around to say good night, Ena finally felt what that lack of empathy. It felt empty to only see a smile and a wave goodbye. People expressed themselves with their bodies, their faces, and their voices. Empathy was the deep fourth way to express what's inside.

When they were good and gone, Ena gave Bogelb another chance to explain what she was going through. She didn't. She was too scared to talk about her secret hope. Whatever Bogelb wanted she was gonna keep it close to the chest. So Ena opened up that great wound that was her for Torno.

Ena told her about listening to the vocal gem broadcasts of the Great Generation, and slowly coming to imagine this handsome outsider named Torno, how she imagined him dancing with her because he didn't care what she looked like. She confessed in a hushed voice, that she'd stolen the Romantic Escape with him and how hurt she'd been when he cheated on Kalta. Talking about working under him as a Broker was difficult, there was too much to explain.

"That entire time you were working with him, you never got over him cheating on Kalta?" Bogelb asked.

"No! Not until I learned the truth and even then I couldn't really admit what was going on in my heart. I still love him. I don't think I ever stopped loving him, and now I don't know if he'll have me." Ena sent out a burst of shame.

It was enough for Bogelb to become forlorn. "Maybe he'll forgive you."

"I don't even think he'll forgive himself." She slid into the booth and tried to hide her face behind her half-finished mug of mead. "What would you do if you were Torno?"

"I don't think I could imagine that."

"But you kind of can. Grou is four years younger than you and that's about the age difference between me and Torno. What if you stayed behind in Schlabaum and spent two years getting to know her? What if you confessed your love for her again and again, and she finally talked you into getting over her? Would you want to take her back?"

Bogelb sent out a pain so sharp Ena grabbed her own chest. "I don't think I could," she admitted. "The thought of confessing my love to her is too much for me. Even one rejection would be too much. Torno must have a head wound to do it more than once. If he stopped trying to win your affection that probably means he's healing. I don't know if it's right to reopen those wounds."

"What if she kissed you?"

Hope. Lust. Shame. Excitement. Queasiness. "I don't know. I don't think that would be any better than her just talking to me. I think if you're going to tell Torno you like him, you can't half-ass it. If you really want to be with him, you need to tell him that this about love. Let him know he's the only man for you."

Ena frowned at that expression. "'The only man for you.' That's a strange way to put it."

"I guess you could try being with a woman." Curiosity.

Blushing, Ena tried to enjoy the mead.

"Really?! Ena, you have to tell me what it was like!"

Embarrassed flames jut out her chest. "Why me?"

"Because Visk won't tell me thing one about her and Duli. The second I bring it up she gets stoic and tight-lipped," Bogelb grumbled.

"Myrrel's been with women," Ena told her. "Her first time was with a woman, if I remember correctly. I think she was a refugee from Duan Si. Maipe. That had to be her name." Ena sent out fond memories of Myrrel telling the tale.

"What happened to her?" Hope.

"She went back to rescue her parents. Myrrel never saw her again."

Bogelb's head sank down. "Why does love always end with loneliness?"

"It begins with loneliness, too. Maybe that's what people are without love."

Bogelb and Ena shared a long drink.

THE FIFTY-EIGHTH CHAPTER

In Which Ena Learns a Name

Dead trees lead the way through Muttur's path. There were no roads that ran this way, and there never had been. Shrubs and saplings promised to restore the forest to its former glory, but they fought Team Freedom's progress every step of the way. The ground was weak, breaking down to loose soil with every step. Torno's schistrau, Zenlauf, had no trouble getting through the weathered terrain so he played the role of scout. He rode from hill to hill as Team Freedom and their horses traversed the mostly flat valley between.

"Hey, Torno." Ena waved him over. "Talk with me."

He eyed her with suspicion. "You need to fit my head to a noose?"

"I will be if you keep this attitude up," she chuckled. "How did you get so good at tracking? I didn't know they taught you that at the High Chantry for Pretentious Assholes."

"I was just good at it."

"No one's 'just good' at anything. I promise not to use this information to tease you later."

His stoicism came away to reveal a tough guard. "When I was really young, my father took me hunting. I can remember him showing me how to follow a path from how a branch snapped, or how to tell where a fight started and ended."

"Your sisters were there too?"

"No, my stepmother forbade them to join us. She thought hunting was men's work. None of us *needed* to hunt. It was just something my dad thought men should know how to do. I used to think it was an excuse for us to get away from my mom. By the time I was maybe seven I learned those trip were really about him visiting a mistress."

"Your mother?"

Torno laughed at the innocent question. "No, my stepmother sent my mother off to Doronel shortly after the Supreme Magus came to power." He thought about it. "I've never told you about her, have I?"

She shook her head and moved closer. The horse and schistrau fought to keep that distance large.

"She was a servant. I think they called them serfs back when your father was king. My father said she was the most beautiful woman he ever laid eyes on, and that he only slept with her once. It always sounded like a lie to me. The only thing I remember about her was how she was always happy to see me. I don't remember her face or even her voice. But when she came back from a shift at work, I was her world. I'd hold tight and listen to her sing."

"Do you remember the song?"

Torno nodded. "Why all the questions all of a sudden?"

Ena shrugged. "Is it so weird that I want to know more about you?"

"I guess not. It is a little unfair that I know everything about you and you know so little about my childhood."

"You do not know everything about me," she protested.

"No? I know the name of the Chantry you trained at. I know the name of your favorite teacher and the one who made you dye your hair black and tried to dye your skin. I can name your five worst bullies. I know how long your parents were in hiding from the democratic revolutionaries and I even remember your story about that little doll that got taken away from you."

"You do *not* know everything about me," Ena insisted.

"Share me something new."

She blushed thinking about the first big secret she wanted

to tell him and the second one made her feel faint.

"What's that? Has the limitless wit of Ena finally wilted?"

She hid her face behind her long black wig.

"No punch? I must've hit a nerve." He let out a comical wince.

"Maybe I haven't told you my secrets for a reason, did you ever think of that?"

He regarded her bashfulness with a natural smile. His face was so handsome it made thoughts turn into a jumble of letters. She loved the way he looked at her when he was playing around. Would they still tease each other when they were lovers? Maybe all of this would change. Maybe he'd never smile at her again as a way of getting back at her for all insults she threw at him. His expression shifted to one of genuine curiosity, but the question died on his tongue.

"Village!" Visk shouted from the ridge of a hill.

"Burned down?" Torno asked. He rode over to Visk.

This was never going to happen as long as things kept pulling Torno away from her. She still wasn't even sure if she *should* say something. Ena wasn't like Torno, she couldn't just blurt out, "I'm in love with you." Of course, the first confession from him hadn't come out that way. He'd looked her in the eyes and struggled to get the words out. Torno had told her that he was becoming obsessed with her. Ena felt pretty obsessed herself.

~ ~ ~

It was a simple village, called Monfel by the locals. The name was supposedly derived from the red flowers that grew among the hillocks, but those red flowers had all burned when Muttur set the forest ablaze. Unlike all of the villages that came before, the villagers responded to Muttur's picture with curiosity. They knew him and they knew him well. Muttur had grown up in Monfel.

Bogelb convinced them that they were worried about

Muttur and they were escorted over to meet his father.

"You're sure they said father?" Visk asked.

"I heard it, too," Ena said. "Did you catch his name, Bogelb?"

"They called him Whisper, but I don't think that's his name. If it is, he must've had some weird parents."

Monfel was one of the smallest villages they'd visited. There were maybe fifty people in town, and all of them lived a fair distance apart. Small hillocks had been made into homes by the hand-crafted doors that market their entrances. Felled trees divided the road from farms. Livestock fences were close enough to the vegetables for stubborn goats to reach out and chew the leaves. Hollowed-out trees had been turned into light posts to mark turns in the road or the end of a property. This was the kind of village that never had any visitors, and they didn't want them either.

Whisper's house was a good deal off the main path. It was immediately recognizable by the colorful pavestones that marked the path up to the small house. On the side of the ankle-high wall were tiny wooden people with bird wings. Real feathers made up the small wings, and every face was cut into an eerie, permanent smile. Each figure had been hand-crafted and was wildly different from the others. Their local guides did not continue down this eerie path, they merely pointed and left without any well wishes.

Masks covered the exterior walls, each of them inhuman. There were masks of Reptear, Marinelds, the pig-faced Slata from Ki'an, and ones with arms on the sides of their faces to represent Boulba. Some of the masks were made to look like trees, or the sun, or mountains. All of them bore a horrifying smile that cut from cheek to cheek. On the door was a metal schistrau face, its beak working as the knocker.

Ena couldn't shake the feeling of dread as she approached the door. This place should be friendly. It should be the kind of place children loved and that parents adored, but something about the artistry spoke not of joy or love or kindness or hope or life. These were faces constructed by a mind that had forgotten what a smile was or why it existed. She looked to her friends for reassurance and they urged her to use the knocker. It clacked down with a hollow sound. No person even a foot away would recognize that sound as anything but a shift in a house brought about by the wind or a change in the temperature.

Yet, the door opened.

He was a sickly, thin man who may have at one point been nine inches over five feet, but the extreme hunch in his back brought him eye level with Ena. On his sunken face sat two glistening orbs of piercing desperation. The cloudy-blue skin of his face tightened and peeled back his hair-thin lips into a parody of delight. But this was no smile, it was a toothy mockery of levity. It was the kind of smile a dying man forced out on his deathbed. It was a grin Ena had only ever seen on the rotten teeth of a Cannegurin.

"Can I help you?" the man asked with a nervous chuckle.

Ena brought out what she considered Torno's best picture. "We're looking for this boy. We were told you knew him?"

"Oh," the man said with that sickly chuckle of recognition. "That's a good likeness for my son. He's been gone for a month and a half now." There was a rattle in his lungs when he laughed. It sounded like it could shift into a life threatening cough or a raspy shout of anger. He stepped back. "You're welcome to come inside, but I'm afraid the Ki'an and the Boulba won't fit. My humble hovel was only built for Lebens."

"I'll wait with them," Myrrel volunteered.

"I'm likely to hit my head," added Torno.

Ena shot a look at them. This was *not* the time to ditch her! But they were already walking back to take in the rest of the village.

Bogelb stepped forward with a smile. "We'll be happy to see your home."

"Excellent." He walked back in tiny shifts of his feet. Those bulging orbs above his taught cheeks never seemed to blink. "I'll get some tea."

"No, thank you," Bogelb said quickly.

It was dark inside. What light entered the front room came in from a connected workshop that had once been a kitchen. There was something dark in the center of the room where a stove or table might've been. Two sofas sat catty-corner from each other, both facing the dark figure. When Ena sank into the sofa it felt like falling into the webs of the Ekeet.

"It is so dark here." The man tried to chuckle apologetically, but it sounded like the hiss of a startled crow. "Let me get the light."

The single candle illuminated the central figure between the couches. It was a life-sized reconstruction of an eight-year-old Leben boy. The child wore simple green clothes, an autumn cap, and a smiling face more somber than any of the masks. His eyes were painted bone-white with little red specks adding fine detail. The statue of the boy had his hands together in prayer, but the proportions of the figure were so skewed that it almost looked like he was about to lunge forward and choke them.

Taking in this horrifying effigy all at once, Ena jumped back.

"That's my late son, Sommech. Isn't he a sweet boy?" the man said.

"I'm sure he was," Ena forced out.

"The Gods took Sommech from us. They lured him into the creek and drowned him. A terrible thing, wouldn't you agree?" He laughed at nothing and it turned into a cough, and for one small instance, a squeal of anger.

"Tragic," Bogelb said. "Sir, where is your wife?"

"Oh." His strained smile loosened into an open-mouthed expression of bewilderment. "They took her, too. She wouldn't smile, you see?" The forced smile was back on his face. "But I don't have that problem, do I?"

"No." Ena cleared her throat. "What's your name, sir? They called you Whisper?"

"You're mistaken. That's what they call my son." His laughter came out like the whine of a fighting cat. "Everyone calls me Happy Hoch."

Bogelb glanced at Ena to show her fraying nerves.

But Ena kept a sociable grace. "Sir, do you mind if I ask you about your wife?"

"She wouldn't smile, you see? That's all you need to know. You should be smiling, too." He reached forward with both hands.

Ena grabbed his wrists. Then she put on a smile and lowered his hands. "I'm fine, Hoch. We both know how to smile."

"Oh, good. The Gods don't like people who can't smile. Cruel as they are, we can't resent them, can we?"

"No," Ena agreed. She kept that smile on her lips and suddenly realized that the man wasn't sending out any empathy. "Hoch, how was your wife when your son was born?"

Despite the permanent smile marring his twisted face, his face pinched inward in rage and his head shook on that gnarled neck of his. "Fine. She was all but fine when she had Gritzen."

"Is that Whisper's given name?" Ena held up the picture of him.

Hoch was staring at Ena's lips, a malicious face shaking as it strained to keep that smile plastered on. Ena tilted her lips slightly and he studied Torno's sketch.

"Yes, that's him. That's my dear sweet Gritzen. It's that butcher boy's fault that he's gone, you know? He taught my sweet boy the sword. He thought he needed to defend himself." He laughed. The laughs were loud as shouts and shook his entire body. "Have you ever heard such a mad thing? Learning the sword to defend oneself!" As laughter shook this wretched man's body, tears squeezed out of those worn-down eyes.

"Who did he have to defend himself against?" Bogelb asked.

"Schuhn, I think his name was. Or was it Swine?" He laughed and cried again. The sound his throat made was overpowering, and it forced them to sit and wait for this fit of emotion to pass. "He's this fat little bully. I asked his father to do something about him, but he wouldn't listen to me. I wasn't strong enough to make him listen." More laughter. It shook his body and forced drool out of those strained lips.

Ena looked to Bogelb. She wanted to get out of there, and Ena couldn't blame her.

"Hoch, we've met your son. Has he always been unable to speak?"

"Oh, yes. He can't hear anything. Why, you could drop a log on someone's head and he wouldn't even turn around!" A mad cackling broke through the thin veneer of civility. "I tried to teach him to move his throat, but he wouldn't have it. Little boys like to bite whatever's put into their mouths, don't they?" His laughter was building into a seething froth.

"Yes." Ena smiled wide. "Little boys are like that."

The look of her smile eased him a little. He wiped at his face and stood to go back to the workspace that was once a kitchen. Every time he moved in or out, he slid more wood shavings about. "I forgot your tea, didn't I?"

"Hoch, were there any changes in your son before he left?"

"Changes? No. No, he's always been the same. He stands there and smiles."

Ena looked to the creepy wooden sculpture of his lost son. "I can see that," she mumbled.

"We should go," Bogelb whispered.

"He could still tell us something about the dreams," she whispered back.

"What was that?" He laughed. "I can't hear whispers! You wouldn't be here to trick me, would you?"

"No, sir. We were just wondering about your son-"

"How is it that you said you knew my Gritzen?" His levity was gone.

The shift from trying to fake a cordial tone to a voice of malice was so sudden that it brought Ena to her feet. He'd returned to the front room with a wooden figurine in his hands. He was whittling away the shape of a head. The knife had no trouble peeling the wood.

"We met him on the road." Ena forced out as much

kindness as she could muster.

"What was he doing? Do he look well?" He sounded less like a man and more like a grindstone that had learned words.

"He was running." Bogelb got between Ena and him; she had to stoop to stand in the small house. "Did he run a lot growing up?"

He tilted his head to think of it. "No. No!" He pointed the wooden chisel at them. "Don't talk to me about Gritzen! He was ruined! They ruined him! I was a good father. It was not my fault that he screamed like that. I never touched him, you hear me?! I never hurt that child!"

Ena backed out of the house.

"No one said you did," Bogelb said.

"I didn't," Hoch muttered. He looked down at the wood figurine and repeated something to himself. The smile slowly slipped back onto his face. A trail of drool drained onto his hands.

Bogelb backed out and closed the door. "Let's get the fuck out of here," she whispered.

Ena nodded.

~ ~ ~

Myrrel held out her hands in inquiry.

"He's mad. He's beyond mad!" Ena gripped her arms, but the shaking wouldn't stop.

"What now? We came all this way, it seems a waste to take off." Torno sighed.

"We're not going to learn anything more from him," Bogelb insisted. "There's a couple people we should follow up with, but I don't even know what we could learn. If the Gods chose the deaf son of that man, they have no mercy in them. We should get out of here and do everything we can to stop Gritzen."

"We can't," Ena insisted. "We need to talk to Schuhn. He's the boy that bullied Muttur growing up."

"He's dead," came the voice of a teenage girl. For a Leben

girl, her Dorospek was exceptional.

She was standing on a hill that was also the roof of a home. Her hair was dyed half red and half blue and twisted together into a topknot. There were two Boulba in armor-helmets standing beside her, and four more Boulba came up from behind Team Freedom from the other side. "His father is dead, too. Gritzen killed them both before he left."

Torno half drew his sword, ready to fight these armored Boulba. "Who are you?"

"I was a friend of Gritzen's growing up. The name's Robla. I've come back to Monfel because I need your help."

Visk imbued her spear with rings of geomantic force. "Why would we help you?"

"Because if you don't, everyone in Monfel is going to die."

"How can you possibly know that?" Myrrel scoffed.

"Lower your weapons," Ena said, gently. "She's a Sage."

Robla nodded. "That's right, and four more Sages are coming."

THE FIFTY-NINTH CHAPTER

When Love is Drowned by Blood

Team Freedom found themselves in the residence of a farmer. It had been the farm of Vogisch, a stoic bitter man feared throughout Monfel, but too important for any to dispel. So when Vogisch fell down a hill, there was no formal investigation. Instead the people of Monfel quietly allowed all of Vogisch's responsibilities to pass to his eldest, Bescheid. He did nothing when his brother Schuhn harassed Gritzen and Robla. Nor did he argue when his father had forced a marriage with Robla's sister Wachla.

Wachla, had married into this family of sadistic farmers. She and her husband were an odd couple. Wachla could've been Robla's twin, save that her hair was a natural black and her husband Bescheid had a round face ill-fitting his broken brow and mostly thin nose. Robla and Wachla sent out thunder clouds of empathy at each other. Ena had seen her fair share of smalltown squabbles and they could last generations, giving rise to village wide divisions if given enough time to fester. Fester was definitely the word for it. Robla wasn't there because she was welcome, she was there because she had nowhere else to go.

Wachla slammed down a covered pot of stew.

"Thank you," Robla told her sister.

Cold poured off Wachla.

Wachla picked two kikaa off the table, tossing them into a pen. There hadn't been enough room for everyone inside, so Team Freedom shared an outdoor patio space with the kikaa.

The fancy head-crested birds had very little respect for the boundaries of their domain. They jumped onto tables, poked their heads into unattended cups, and wouldn't be scared off. Bescheid dropped off a handful of bowls. He placed them down in a civil but not cordial manner and tried to mollify his wife's wrath with a hand on her back. She had none of it and raged her way back into her house. The man scooped up two more kikaa and the rest followed. Yet the moment he went back into the house, nearly a dozen kikaa jumped over their fence to steal food off the table.

"Ask whatever questions you need, Ena, but we must hurry," Robla told them.

"Who are these four Sages that are coming? Why would they destroy Monfel?"

"They're two Ki'an warriors, a Boulba, and a Slata. I don't know their names, but I've been calling them The Brutals. They serve Galtur, the God of Evil that chooses Hultur. They are coming here, I'm certain of this. Have you met the Dreamers?"

"They've been a mixed bag of pompous and clueless," said Myrrel with a snort.

Robla asked Visk, "Do the people of Ki'an have something like a Dreamer?"

Visk gave a deep nod. "The Hularad live to find the next Hultur and prepare him for conquest. They are vile witches who whisper lies into the ears of Zular and poison their sisters to gain power. In my homeland of the Diamond Sands, their order is not tolerated, but their ilk are uncovered in every generation. These four come from the Hularad?"

Robla nodded. "I think so. They kill innocents and spill their guts to divine the future."

"That is their way," Visk confirmed.

A flash of Ena's dream came back to her. The two Ki'an that killed Haenir had disemboweled him. Her dream about those women had been prophecy. She tried to remember what they looked like, but it had been so long back.

"How did you know Muttur?" Myrrel corrected herself

with a shake of her head. "I mean Gritzen, sorry."

"As I said before, I grew up with him. He was an outcast. Gritzen only went outside at night, when his father slept. I would see him outside and I started sneaking out to talk to him. I taught him how to read and write and how to make faces. I thought I could teach him to speak." It pained her to talk about this. She could barely meet their eyes.

"You fell in love with him," Ena guessed.

She nodded. "He wasn't a wicked boy. Any time something was hurt or in trouble, Gritzen wanted to help. That's how Schuhn came to hate him. Schuhn would kick around the kikaa when Gritzen stood up to him. Schuhn threw him into the pen with the kikaa and he kept doing that pushing back in until they'd hurt him."

Ena had been too focused on Robla. She didn't notice the kikaa pulling her bowl of stew off the table. It poured over Ena's side. The kikaa jumped off the table and pecked at her scraps.

"We mean to kill him," Visk told Robla.

She nodded, letting her head droop and her eyelids flutter shut. "I know."

Ena tried to clean the mess at her side. "Do you know if we succeed?"

"I know that I don't survive to find out," said Robla.

Clearing his throat, Torno eased the tone a smidge. "Tell us about how he killed Schuhn."

"It had been building up for a long time. Schuhn and his brothers would beat Gritzen and he'd stay hidden. But he wouldn't ever stay away. Schuhn would start courting me or someone would tease me and he'd run out to try and intervene. Grtizen was always my hero, but Schuhn saw me as his property. His mother and mine promised us to each other when we were very young. When I refused the Dance of Promise, my sister was promised to Bescheid instead."

They looked into the house.

"I take it she's not happy with her husband," Myrrel guessed.

Robla shook her head. "Bescheid was the sweetest of his brothers. She hates me for...other reasons.

"Regardless, Gritzen and Schuhn hated each other. No matter what Schuhn did to him, Gritzen was there for me. Eventually Schuhn tried to beat the courage out of Gritzen. He was beated so bad that he pissed blood. After that...he...he stopped going outside. I tried to get him to come out again by having a little picnic under a tree he could see from his window. Schuhn saw me and...Well, he grabbed me and forced me to kiss him. He told me he was going to make me marry him. I think Gritzen saw us and he stopped coming to the window.

"A friend of ours, Salfe, told me that he could teach Gritzen how to fight. I had been thinking of myself as Ngoltur and he as my Muttur, and I...pushed Gritzen into it. I snuck into Gritzen's home and physically pulled him outside. I was screaming at his father for keeping him in there like that. It hadn't been the first time we'd fought. Anyway, I talked Gritzen into learning how to fight. I thought that even if he didn't want to defend me, it would be good for him. It was something he didn't need a voice to do well. But the night before he was supposed to learn how to fight, he changed.

"He didn't come outside to see me and learn letters, and when I asked his father about Gritzen, he said he had fallen into a deep sleep. His dad let me come inside and see for myself."

"When was this?" Sal asked.

Robla told him the date. It was the day they'd all arrived in Leben Erde.

Team Freedom shared glances but no one voiced their suspicions.

Robla continued her story. "Gritzen woke up changed. He came outside early in the morning and ran around town without fear. He was running up to everyone and talking to them. Well, he would stand by them and try to read their lips. He never did that before. He started training with Salfe right away. Salfe said that he took to swordplay fast. Within an hour he broke Salfe's fingers in a sparring match.

"Things had gotten bad with Schuhn. He was dragging me around by the hand and I had to kiss him whenever he asked. If I didn't..." Robla clasped her hands together so tight that her knuckles turned white.

"You don't have to tell us how he hurt you," Myrrel assured her.

She closed her eyes and nodded. "I'm sorry."

"Don't be." Myrrel leaned over to rub her back. "Nothing that happened was your fault."

"I mean about telling the story. This is my destiny and I can barely get through it." The fifteen-year-old girl was shaking.

"Robla, this hasn't been easy for any of us," Ena assured her. "If it's too hard to tell us about Gritzen killing Schuhn, that's fine. We said that we would help you, right? What do you need us to do?"

"You need to get Monfel to evacuate. The Brutals are coming. They will kill my family when they arrive, but I can't convince them to leave. I can't even talk my neighbors into leaving!" Tears spread a creak down her indigo cheeks. She choked back a sob and swore in Faulchet.

Torno handed her a handkerchief.

Robla wiped her face, but it didn't help.

Ena regarded the Boulba accompanying her. They sat a measured distance from the table, accepting what was said has little to do with them. They were here to defend Robla from these Brutals she feared. "What does she think we should do?"

A gray slate Boulba raised up the visor of his helmet-armor. "If you announce yourself as Ngoltur they'll listen to you. Please follow her request. I know that serfs shouldn't command queens, but that girl has suffered greatly to be here. She grew up with these people."

Ena sought council from Team Freedom. "What are we risking?"

"Tell me you're not thinking about leaving the people of Monchel behind?" Myrrel asked.

"I'm thinking about raising fortifications and fighting the

Brutals here. I don't like the sound of these Sages and I want to put a stop to them. My blood is hot. I need to know what's at stake."

"Kalta might find us," Torno said as if it wasn't that big of a threat.

"I am with you, Ena." Visk raised her chin with pride. "We should stay behind and meet these Hularad in battle."

"No!" Robla flailed her hands between them. "You mustn't! If you try to fight The Brutals, they will kill you all and take Ena! I've seen it in my dreams."

"Ena is very powerful and I am no stranger to fighting Hularad," Visk assured the girl.

"It doesn't matter." Robla gave out a sigh of frustration.

"The Sages see the future," Sal reminded her. "If one Sage can foresee a coming danger, four might be able to foresee a conflict in perfect detail."

Ena thought about Sylene and her clairvoyant powers. "Especially if they have dream magic."

Robla nodded emphatically.

"If that's the case, isn't all of this pointless?" Myrrel asked. "These people can predict our every move, right?"

"The future isn't set," Ena explained. "They can only predict where I'm going as long as I have one plan of action. Robla coming here is changing the outcome. What is it these Brutals want?"

"I don't know," Robla admitted with a tired sigh. "I'm sorry."

"The Hularad want one thing: death." Visk straightened her back to emphasize the severity of the threat before them. "They sleep with bones and bathe in blood. If they have come to Leben Erde then they are looking for Hultur."

Ena thought about the metaphor with the cups moving from hand to hand. "No, Hultur means nothing to them. He's been blessed with Wisdom. Gritzen was chosen by Varn, or Galtur, or whatever its true name is. The, uh, God that usually selects Hultur. If these four Sages are as competent as the Grand

Dreamer, they'll be looking for Gritzen."

Torno snapped and slammed his fist into his palm. "This is how he takes over the world; with the help of these four Sages."

"What's this about him taking over the world?" asked the gray slate Boulba.

"I'm sorry," Robla said. "This is Colonel Armside. He's been helping me since I got to Karzak."

Myrrel showed her kudos. "I'm impressed you got to Karzak by yourself."

She lowered her head.

"Her friend Salfe joined her and they picked up four others on the road. Robla was the only one who made it to Karzak alive," Colonel Armside explained. "I've lost four of mine getting her back here. I meant it when I said she's been through a lot."

"Okay, I've heard enough." Ena stood. "They basically have an evil Team Freedom. The longer we wait around, the harder it's going to be to outrun them. Torno, Visk, you two tell Colonel Armside everything he needs to know. Myrrel, I need you to make me look as imperial as you possibly can. Bogelb, I wanna punch up my speech with an empathy whammy I need you council on how to send empathy out to a crowd. Sal, I want you to search the graveyard."

"What am I looking for?"

"My gut tells me there's a murderer here and I'll be damned if I let anyone get away with killing someone. Check the tombstones for Gritzen and Schuhn's family and investigate their bones. Questions?"

Team Freedom shook their heads.

"Good." She clapped her hands like Torno used to do. "Let's go save this village."

THE SIXIETH CHAPTER
In Which a Ruler Commands

Ena barely recognized the woman in the mirror. She was adorned in a big frilly skirt and a bodice that pressed down on her chest and left too much room around her hips. Her natural pink skin looked strange after seeing herself in blue for so long and her short off-yellow hair looked stranger still. It had grown out past her ears but still wasn't long enough to tame with fancy braids. Yet all of that was cosmetic. The biggest change to Ena's appearance was something deeper.

She was so used to seeing a scared girl, a young woman who was unsure of herself. Even back on her twentieth birthday she'd been unsure about what her place was in the world. Now she was a leader. She was a killer too. The idea of facing four Sages didn't scare her. Even the idea of fighting Gritzen again didn't scare her. She was ready for what was coming.

"You look beautiful," sighed Robla's sister, Wachla.

Ena smiled. It looked forced on her lips, but at least her smile looked human. "Thank you. Is everyone ready for me?"

"They are. Are you really siding with my sister and telling everyone to leave?" Wachla asked.

"You have to."

"But this is our home."

Ena gently took the arms of this scared woman. "Wachla, this is the only way you can save your family. Do you love Bescheid?"

"Of course!" She rubbed her belly. She didn't show any signs of being pregnant, but something about the gesture made it clear that she was. "I want to raise a family with him."

"Then help me convince them to leave. Tell me what they need to hear."

Wachla shook her head. "I don't think anything could make us leave. I don't know if I'd want to live anywhere but Monfel. Not even if you paid me. Not even if you told me that I'd be coming to live in your palace, Your Wisened."

Ena didn't bother to correct her words and blushed when the woman curtsied.

She left Ena with her head held low.

Adjusting her magical bracelets, fingering her casting rings, she steadied her breathing and considered the shape of the spells she need to cast. This was going to be more than a speech, it was a magical performance. Walking out to meet the gathered crowd, Ena's jaw was too stiff to suck in a breath. Everyone in Monfel was there, even that creepy toymaker, Hoch.

Sal and Myrrel came to Ena's side. "Well?"

"The fracture on Schuhn's father suggests a blow to the skull," Myrrel confirmed.

"I didn't find anything wrong with Gritzen's mother or brother," said Sal. "What are you going to do?"

She shook her head. "I don't know. These people don't want to leave."

"Ena, how did you know someone was murdered?" Sal asked.

"Something Gritzen's father said. I think I'm getting better at reading people or something. For all I know it's part of my divine power." She shook her head. "Are we all ready to leave?"

"Yeah, Torno has everything packed up." Myrrel looked up at the darkening sky. "You sure we'll make it back to that town by nightfall?"

"No, but we'll be back before the sun rises." She shrugged. "Is Robla ready to go?"

"She said she won't leave without her people," Sal told her.

Ena gave a long sigh. "Try talking to Armside, something tells me he'll be able to talk some sense into her."

Sal left with haste, using his long arms to move quickly.

Myrrel leaned in to fix her makeup. "You're nervous."

"You know what small villages are like. The place doesn't even have a road in and out of town. They don't think about the world beyond these hills. I won't be able to convince them to abandon their lives."

"Just remember, whoever decides to leave with you is a life that would've died. Give up on convincing everyone and work to save as many as you can." It was good advice coming from a healer. That had to be how Myrrel kept so calm when bodies were laid before her.

"Okay."

Myrrel gave her a firm hug. It lasted far longer than something casual.

Ena leaned into the embrace, letting it last as long as Myrrel wanted. When it ended, Ena asked, "What was that for?"

"I'm so proud of you, Camellia."

"Thank you." Ena took a swig from Narla's flask and went out to make a speech.

There was a makeshift platform on a hill. She walked through some of the crowd, lifting her skirt as she went. When they saw her they gasped and gossiped, but many of them were skeptical, and more still shot Robla dirty looks. Raising her hands, Ena sent out a warm breeze of happiness. Ena tapped the voice gem affixed over the hollow of her throat and it glowed to life, ready to amplify her voice.

"I am Ngoltur Reborn. I have come here because the Gods have new plans for me. Though I was born a Princess, my lands were taken from my parents, and my crown was melted down for coins. Still the Gods have not given up on me. They have sent me to Leben Erde to help Monfel. There is a danger coming and it threatens to kill you all."

Ena bit her lip and thought of Narla dying in her arms. The fear washed over her, and she spread that fear out to the crowd. She sent it out like the indigo film of the balebog and let it pour down on them.

"You are not safe here. You haven't been safe here." She sent out thoughts of the Ki'an women pulling Haenir out to disemboweling him. "Schuhn beat Gritzen and you did nothing. He dragged Robla around like property and you did nothing. He would've raped her on her wedding night and you would've done nothing."

She went back to the thought of Narla's death. She held onto that feeling of complete failure and powerlessness at the sight of her death. She failed Narla, just as these people failed their neighbors. She assaulted them with that sensation.

"None raised a hand to stop him because you refused to see the corruption in your own home. You chose to believe a lie that your home was a castle that none could break down! And any that challenged that narrative were silenced!"

Ena had plenty of shame to draw on. All she needed to do was think about how she was manipulating them. It was hard to draw on that shame without pulling from her own disgust. Still, maybe it wouldn't be so bad if there was some guilt thrown in.

"This is not safe! Vogisch was killed. Murdered by one of your own, and you knew about it!"

It was a guess and a gamble, but as her eyes swooped over the crowd not all could meet her gaze. She poured out whatever suspicion and fear she could grab.

"Still, none have come forward. You live with a murderer and think this is fine because it is better to live with lies than to admit the truth that Monfel is not a sanctuary. Your town was named for the red flowers that grow on your hills, but look around! All the poppies have burned. The time to leave has come."

She drew on her disgust at herself and cast a bolt of lightning into the sky. It was thicker than she was wide and spread out over the sky, resonating with the clouds above. Thunder thoomed and echoed as more lightning rallied to her call. The people jolted back and the rain came.

"That is a fraction of the power I wield. That is that kind of danger you face by staying here. You may choose to stay and die here. You may think that it is a great purpose to fight and preserve the legacy of your great village, but this was never a great village. You lived here because you believed in a lie. Do not die to keep that lie alive. Leave! Leave or you will die for nothing!"

Ena's fancy dress was soaking through, clinging to her skin as she walked down the hill.

Sal stood beside Robla, a look of absolute horror on both their faces.

"Are you coming with us?" Ena snapped at Robla.

Fearfully, she nodded.

"Good." She strolled into the Gyeterl—a boulba drawn cart.

Their stuff was all inside. The size and feel of the wagon was all wrong. She crossed her arms and sank to her knees. One by one the wagon filled up with Team Freedom and Ena couldn't meet their eyes. She wanted to cry. She wanted to scream in rage and tear off the dress to expose her twisted heart. She looked to her friends and they met her eyes with worry.

"I want you all to promise me something. When all of this is done, don't let me become the ruler of a nation. If I wear a crown by the time this over, kill me."

"Ena, no!" snapped Torno.

"I mean it! You saw what I did. You felt the force of my empathy magic worked onto that crowd. If I controlled a country like that, who could oppose me? Who could even think to speak out against me? You have to promise me that you won't let me turn into a leader of a nation. All of you. Swear it to me on your life or leave this team and live a long happy life away from me."

Visk knelt to attention as high as the wagon would allow. She struck her heart with her fist. "I swear it."

Sal ran his hands over his face. "Fine. I swear it. I swear it with my last breath."

"I don't think it's my place to promise something like that," said Bogleb.

"Bogleb, you're part of this now. If you're going to keep

traveling with me, you have to be willing to put your life on the line," Ena growled. She wasn't letting any of them back down from this.

"I'll do everything I can to make sure you never become a Queen or any other kind of ruler," Bogelb promised.

"I won't live long enough to change what's coming." Robla's voice was strained from crying. "But what you did was horrible. I've never felt empathy magic like that, it was something suffocating, like you were drowning everyone. You may have saved their lives, but they will never feel safe for as long as they live."

"Probably not," Ena agreed.

Robla had plenty of hatred for Ena but she wouldn't speak the words. Full of a regret for the power she unleashed, she bowed her head and went back to crying.

"I don't want to promise that, Ena," Myrrel said. "I refuse to take a life. I'm not a warrior. I never have been."

"Then you need to leave us."

"Ena!" Torno snapped.

"Now, wait one minute," shouted Sal.

"No!" Ena shouted back at them. "This isn't a game. Narla is dead. Robla is ready to die. We're all ready to die, but it's not enough to be ready to die. We have to be ready to kill. If Myrrel's actions mean the difference between Gritzen dying and him killing one of us, I *need* to know that I can count on her."

"Fuck you," Myrrel grumbled.

"Myrrel-"

"I'll do it, okay?!" The furry of her expulsion staggered her. Leaving her eyes distant as tears rolled down her cheeks. "I'll kill him. I'll kill a fifteen-year-old boy that never had a fucking chance. I'll kill a boy who knew nothing but pain and suffering because he'll do a thousand times worse if he's allowed to keep living. Alright?! I'll turn into the cold, heartless monster Narla spent the last twenty years of her life trying to stop being! I'll turn into a killer because that's what we need.

"Because I love you, Ena! I love you..." She grit her teeth

and choked back tears. "Like you're my own sister! I am not going to walk away from you. I will not leave you because you're scared of losing us. If you need me to kill, then I'll do it. But I'm telling you now, Ena, I'm not going to warn you. If I think that you're going to be worse than Gritzen, if I think that you're going to be the leader of anything more than us, I won't give you a warning."

It was strange how Myrrel's promise eased the weight on Ena's shoulders. She felt a smile spread on her face. "Thank you."

Myrrel looked away in disgust.

All that was left was Torno. She needed him to make this promise. If he told her "no," Ena didn't think she had the strength to kick him out of the group.

Torno seemed to rest on this edge of frustration and futility and his voice was weak from the effort. "Ena, I still don't think you will be a bad leader."

"It doesn't matter, Torno!" she snapped back. "You saw what I did out there! You felt what I pushed on them. Everything we're doing right now is to preserve the concept of self-governance. If I have the power to supersede my will onto others, then all of the decisions they make aren't their own. I can't be allowed to use that power on a populace!"

"Even if you're right?" he snapped back.

"Yes! People need to have the right to make mistakes!"

"You didn't force those people to leave their home. So what if you pushed your will onto them, so what if you pulled at their heartstrings? Public speakers have been doing that since we first had language. The fact that you added magic to your words doesn't change that. They might be chilled to the bone by your speech, but they won't be able to leave overnight. When those people wake up, they're going to think, 'she's wrong.'

"I know these people. I've seen how they think. I can lecture them about the right thing until my throat is hoarse from screaming and they'll be nodding the entire time. But you know what happened after our wagon left. They stayed the same. You are not responsible for the death of their sense of security. You do not have the power to control people. Not even the Gods have that power. If they did, none of this would've been possible.

"We're not fighting for an ideology. Free will doesn't need us to fight for it. We're fighting to keep one man from leading a psychotic order to conquer the world. That's it. We cannot control the minds of anyone. You don't have that power. You don't have that responsibility!"

She wanted to leap across that wagon, wrap her arms around him and kiss him. She could feel her cheeks pulling back into a smile. She leaned back against the wagon's scratched tarp and nodded. "Okay."

Torno blinked. "Really?"

"Yeah. You're right. You're right too, Myrrel. I'm sorry. I shouldn't have tried to control you like that."

"No, you shouldn't have," she sniffed.

Ena crawled over and hugged her. "I'm sorry." This quiver in her heart wouldn't relent but hugged tighter let the tears flow. "I'm sorry, Myrrel."

"It's okay." She hugged Ena back. "It's alright. I know you're trying to do the right thing, but you can't...We're not your hands."

"I know." Ena looked to Visk. "I'm sorry I ordered you like that, Visk. And I love that you'd do that for me. I love that all of you would kill me if I asked you to. I'm so confused. I'm so scared of losing you."

"Do not be afraid to die," Visk told her with a stern face. "Be afraid that you will die without living."

"That's easy for you to say," Robla mumbled.

"You accept your fate because death is easy," Visk told her. "A warrior does not serve Death, a warrior commands Death. I have seen a hundred battles and those who share your eyes do not survive. Living is a great challenge. Will you rise to the challenge like a woman, or will you await your death like a child?"

Fear gripped her. It shook her head and made her look away from Visk, but Ena found those fearful eyes. Ena wasn't content to let the young Robla give up.

"The four Sages haven't found me yet because I continue to change who I am," Ena told her. "Even the Gods could not control what I did. We can change our fates, Robla."

"Then I will try to live."

Visk stood up, stooping her back to keep from poking her head through the top. She held out her hand. Robla gave this tall Ki'an warrior her demure hand and Visk pulled her up. "Women rise to all challenges. What are you?"

"A woman," she whispered.

"What are you?"

"A woman!" she shouted.

"Men do okay," Torno muttered to Sal.

"Yeah, we do alright," he agreed.

Ena laughed at the pair of them. She threw herself at Torno and hugged his shoulders. He returned the hug with only one arm but it was enough. She wanted to melt into his arms and shower him with kisses. This would have to do for now. "Thank you."

Torno shook his head. "All that came from you."

"So we have an Archmage trying to kill us, four evil Sages are going to try to thwart our plan, Gritzen is collecting powerful relics, and we don't know where Hultur is," Sal said, listing them off on his giant fingers.

Smiling, Ena nodded. "That's about right."

"How come you're not afraid of that?" Bogelb asked her.

She shrugged. "Because you'll be here with me when we meet them."

"Wait, what's this about an Archmage?" Robla asked.

They sighed and groaned and explained to the Sage what she was getting pulled into. Ena watched them all in silence. Torno squeezed Ena's shoulders. He was still holding onto her and he was content to be there for her. Lovers or not, he still cared about her. They all did. They were here because they loved her. Pushing them away wasn't going to give her the strength to do what she needed, they were a source of strength for her.

Without them she'd turn into everything she feared. No matter what happened, Ena was done fantasizing about them leaving her to start their own lives. This was their life and Ena was going to live it without fear.

The Twisting the Turall saga will continue.

Book 5
Sages

www.ingramcontent.com/pod-product-compliance
Lightning Source LLC
Chambersburg PA
CBHW060645260626
47161CB00008B/3005